By Derek Meyler

Variations

The Irishman's Journey to Montana

The House on St. Bonaventure Road

THE HOUSE ON ST. BONAVENTURE ROAD

BY DEREK MEYLER

ISBN-13: 9798667312819

To Claudia

It is not for us to understand. It is for us to travel to the very edge of the light we are given. AND THEN? And then we jump with swords drawn, a battlecry on our lips, and we beat back the darkness.

— JENELLE LEANNE SCHMIDT,

Minstrel's Call, (Stormcave, 2018)

AUTHOR'S NOTE

This is a novel based on true events. Yes, such creations do exist. A 'tour de force' by any author in the world of genres, if you will. A regular affair of this and the previous century; combining writer's narrative with truth. A novel in this instance, in the telling of this story, was poignantly imperative to protect in every feasible manner, the identities of the principal protagonists engaged within the crux of this book.

Further to that, the main characters' names have been altered as has the address of the location where the events occurred. Thus, the book's title. The general whereabouts and existence of businesses mentioned herein are accurate as of the time in which the events took place, with the exception of the primary character's firm's location. All place names visited by the chief participants within, are fact-based. Some Christian names (first names) of those on the periphery yet essential to this story, have not been revised and are in fact their actual forenames.

Certain notations in the diary of the central character in this book have been of immense value and I thank him for his fortitude in sharing them with me. Dates have been modified for the most decisive part of this story. I hereby present to you the reader, an account of extraordinary and shocking events that occurred over thirty years ago, engulfing five young adults in Dublin, Ireland. Their response to their predicament was arguably even more remarkable. I give you, in essence, an historical novel.

— Derek Meyler
Wexford
June, 2020

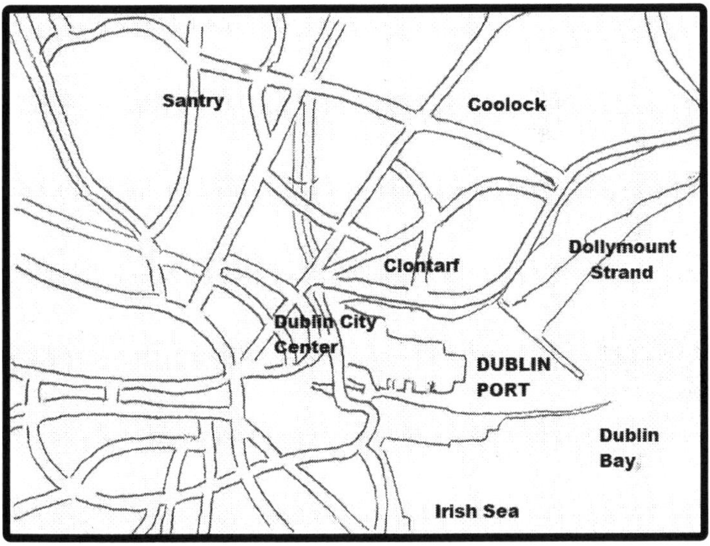
Santry
Coolock
Dollymount
Strand
Clontarf
Dublin City
Center
DUBLIN
PORT
Dublin
Bay
Irish Sea

CHAPTER ONE

MARCH, 2014.

The water-filled potholes displayed little mercy as the Volvo sped on, spluttering through the uneven street. Twilight had descended, enveloping the grey car within its mist of light rain and failing light. That time of evening that occupies the hiatus between day and night along the coasts of Ireland can be detrimental in so many ways. Especially on the Clontarf coastal road, with its high-end residences on one side, the sea wall separating the Irish Sea from the inhabitants of Dublin on the other. Eddie O'Leary kept driving, his passenger silent. Traffic was light. The winds appeared uneasy. Darkness would soon be upon the old city. Taking a sharp, fast and hard left onto St. Bonaventure Road, Eddie, easing his foot off the pedal proceeded up the tree-lined avenue, moving slowly away from Dublin Bay, cautiously.

"What number is it?"

"I told you Eddie, I'm not sure."

"Ah, Jaysus, you must remember, c'mon it's not that long ago, well not that long anyway."

"It is thirty years ago Eddie, for God's Sake!"

"Well, how do I know where to stop; what side of the street is it on?"

"The left side."

"Is it far up, this is one long, very long street I can tell ya?!" Eddie O'Leary was a taxi driver. A veteran of the highways and byways of the city of Dublin, you might say. He knew every one-way street in this vast metropolis. Every nook and cranny. He had contacts everywhere. His geographical knowledge and know-how were legendary. If a patron required the best place in Dublin for haberdashery, Eddie would get him there; sometimes just a small little alleyway in the bowels of Ireland's capital. The best restaurant for lamb? Eddie could zip you across the city to a petite Greek hideaway, which only the 'chosen few' could possibly know. "So Dave, are you going to tell me where to pull up, I'm dying to see this place, ah c'mon you already agreed to show me." Dave looked to the floor, then, within the darkness of the car slowly raised his head. In an unsteady tone he said, "Number 189."

"Hard to see the address numbers, the pathways up to the houses are so long."

"That's ok Eddie, just about 3 more gardens on the left." They slowly came to a halt outside the house. Night had arrived; the big Sycamore trees shuddered in the wind, the protracted pathway up to the house looked ominous, the grass on either side of it dark; foreboding. St. Bonaventure Road, still and quiet. Eddie turned off all lights and extinguished the bulb of his overhead taxi sign. He didn't want anyone or anything disturbing this moment.

The pedestrian gate was closed. They stared up the pathway. The curtains were drawn in the front bay window. The residence appeared dark and sinister yet there was a beckoning about it. "How do you feel being back here?" asked Eddie. A silence ensued. "I don't want to talk about it," replied Dave, as he continuously kept his eyes firmly on the house. "We've known each other for a long time Dave, if you want to talk about it go ahead, I know it must be difficult for ya, but well, this is some moment isn't it? I'm glad after all these years you finally told me the whole story back in the pub tonight, Jesus Christ, that scared the hell out of me!" Unexpectedly, without uttering a word Dave stepped out of the Volvo and approached the closed gate. Standing at its periphery he looked straight beyond it to the front door. 'Still painted black,' he thought. Eddie joined him. "Christ it's spooky in there, even past this gate." Dave turned and got back in the car. Eddie quickly followed. "Let's get the fuck out of here Eddie." "Now!"

Soon clear of the scene, they returned to the working-class Dublin district of Coolock where they had grown up together as neighbours, leaving behind the middle-class manicured lawns, leafy domains and refined distinctive tree-lined avenues and houses designed in the late Victorian era at Clontarf. "When are you heading back, Dave, what day is your flight?"

"On Thursday at 11:30, I'll have to be out at the airport by about half past nine, I guess."

"I'll drop you there no problem on Thursday morning."

"That's grand Eddie, I'll spend tomorrow my last day with my mother here in Coolock. We'll go out on the town you and me for a few scoops of the hard stuff tomorrow night." As he lay in bed later that evening, Dave's thoughts wandered back, almost reluctantly, to 189 St. Bonaventure Road. 'God, I shouldn't have let him talk me into going back there.' Memories came sweeping back, flooding him with angst, the shadowy corners of his mind beset with horror; a clouded compendium of remembrances opening up into a reservoir of ghastly occurrences swirling about in his brain, tormenting him, returning it to him, terrifying him. He knew such things can exist; he had witnessed it firsthand. Banishing all memory of those events for the last 30 years for the most part, it was as if he had given himself a directive to obliterate that chapter in his life from all mention. An erasure of the truth, in a sense. Society, for all its virtues, for all its nuances, for all its claims of understanding, its self-help groups and open discussion forums, were nothing but pure garbage to Dave in relation to 'the unknown.' For society's tolerance wears thin, perhaps because of a fear of the standard norms being whisked away, right down to a refusal to accept that there are other worlds, more profusely other dimensions within the universe, separated by a mere thread or indeed, beyond the grave! That evil itself can be an integral portion of the mysteries of the universe and be intertwined within such concepts is anathema to most. Dave knew that. He had that declaration to himself to protect his person, his mind from ridicule. He would soldier on. The only manner he could conduct that would be in the eradication of it all. Just get on with daily life. But in the essence of things, does not all come full circle? Now so many years had passed and he had been confronted again with the truth. The terror subsiding, lying there in his bed, his mind wandered back to the days of his youth, his wild and crazy youth in Dublin, his longing for a better life that by hook or by crook, would lead him on to new beginnings across the water and ultimately, paradoxically...189 St. Bonaventure Road.

NOVEMBER, 1982.

The boisterous clinking of glasses surrounded him as he sat with his mates in Slattery's Pub of Capel St. in Dublin City Centre. Up on the stage in the tiny lounge/

bar on the 1st. Floor were 'The Jolly Beggarmen,' playing their folk tunes and Irish ballads for the benefit of the regular patrons that came here every Saturday night, come hell or high water, come snow, rain or golden summer evenings. Everyone knew their own table, a simple automatic exercise in arriving at an opportune time and grabbing it without melodrama or fanfare. By 10pm the place would be in an uproar; an emphatic joyous unrestrained continuous rendition of young men and women throwing themselves musically at the feet of the band, as they belted out their numbers without break or pause, one after the other, of Irish Republican rousing ballads stirring patriotic battle even within the breasts of the most faint-hearted. The beer would be flowing and the conversations often fluid and inane.

Embedded inside this setting was Dave Molloy, an intrinsic component of the group at the table. Sometimes up to eleven of them. Always the same faces, the same close friends. Squashed together at a table for six. Grab a chair. Charlie, Tommy, Dessie, Paddy, Martina, Ita, Ann, Geraldine, Karen and Dave's best friend, Johnny. Month after month, year after year they came on Saturday nights to Slattery's. If one of them was missing there would be an inquiry. An inquisition! Who knows what? Where was he? Why don't you know?! A tight knit group. But did Dave belong in this auspicious gathering? He did, though he began to doubt it. Johnny and Martina were now engaged, Charlie and Geraldine were following suit, Ann would soon be off to Italy and Dessie and Karen recently had their nuptials. And to top it off, Paddy had done a disappearing act! All was not the same. Soon families would develop, children would play, Saturday nights at Slattery's would evaporate. 'The natural run of things,' thought Dave. Indeed he was right. And he had no qualms nor complaints. He loved Johnny like a brother and was happy for him and Martina. As he was for the rest. But trouble and heartbreak had been rising in Dave's life and this, his only outlet, seemed to be waning into the sunset. Combining with everything, it clouded his judgment.

Employment was scarce in early 1980's Ireland as Dave deposited his bicycle at the bottom of Dunluce Road to commence his postal delivery up one side and down the other. Sack upon his back, he climbed over railings, in and out of gates, crept into Mr.O'Halloran's front garden tiptoeing between the hedging in his daily attempt to elude the 'lunatic mongrel,' as he named it, that O'Halloran often omitted to lock up when the milkman or postman would arrive. Always on the lookout for the Postal Inspector who loved nailing Postmen's minor infringements, Dave ploughed on with his route. Day after day, week after week, Dave carried the mail to the good citizens of Dunluce Road and environs and you could track his movements and timing to the letter, if you so wished, something which bothered Dave immensely. He was a free spirit at heart, not one for regulations or bureaucracy which was rife and pervaded the entire system he worked for. But where else could he go? What else was available to do? Dave firmly believed there was no gainful employment in Dublin then, that paid well for a working- class fellow like himself. His delivery complete, it was home to his parent's house for some breakfast and a little respite before resuming his duties in the afternoon. Every week he would donate his share of his earnings to the upkeep of his Father and Mother's household where he resided with his younger sisters and brother. With no lady friend currently in his life and the monotony of his existence in continuous motion, all seemed indifferent yet uniform. Until the day he ran into Eric.

In January of 1983 while walking home from a quiet midweek night-time drink, Dave and Eddie came upon a young lad being set upon by a couple of Dublin street thugs. As they rushed to his rescue, Dave sustained some injuries to his neck and soon found himself in St. Vincent's Hospital for a few days treatment. In the bed adjoining him was Eric. A flamboyant character in his mid-thirties with a guitar by his bedside, Eric would regale Dave with tales of his adventures in Latin America and the United States. Mexico was Eric's forte as he spoke of playing his guitar in the streets of Mexico City to enraptured senoritas, all taking to the 'Hombre de Irlanda;' claiming he was a novelty in that part of the world. He would talk of Acapulco and making his way through the Mexican desert and across the Rio Grande to the United States, where Eric stated he settled for a while in Flagstaff, Arizona before making his way to the Pacific Coast and San Diego. Then, just to validate his experiences to Dave, he'd strum away with a combination medley of *'By The Time I Get To Phoenix,' 'El Paso.' 'The Yellow Rose of Texas'* and *'La Bamba!'*

This was enough for Dave. Not necessarily taking Eric's anecdotes at face value, there was an inspiration evolving. Eric had ignited something in Dave; he had reminded him of a whole new world out there, of a freedom of expression that is inherent in all of us by the actions available to us; that we do not have to encase ourselves in a regulatory blindness of the soul. There is more than daily wearisome repetition when your friends are dispersing through the natural processes of life; the family home is no longer your home; the constant postal delivery is not your destiny. Your calling is what you make it, what your instinct tells you, where one can step over the threshold and into their fate.

Indifference had taken a plunge. Dave Molloy had made a decision. A life-altering decision. He would leave behind all that he knew, the culture he was raised in, the dreams of a wife and family in his own country, even his beloved Slattery's. The road ahead and where it would lead appeared liberating and to an extent, definitive. But life can conjure up a satire of cruelty, a barbarous irony. Dave Molloy was headed right into it. He had taken a step closer to the horror that would be 189 St. Bonaventure Road.

CHAPTER TWO

JUNE, 1983.

Field Research Corporation could be quite an engaging and bustling place. Rows and rows of enlivened souls chattering away on their headsets, all juxtaposed in such close proximity that just hearing the answers of your respondent could be a very difficult assignment in itself. This was the environment in which Dave maneuvered Monday to Friday from 1pm to 9pm. Except, Dave was a Coder. He worked upstairs. One floor below him the men and women in the tiny cubicles conducted Market Research on behalf of Mervin Field, the owner. The building lay in the heart of the Financial District of San Francisco. Dave had made it. He had remained steadfast and determinedly, proceeded. The company was willing to teach him coding in the fast-paced world of Political Polls and Market Research. He seemed like a bright young fellow so they gave him a chance. But he would have to learn quickly to retain the position. Such was the business and thinking of the United States free market. Dave loved that. 'Back home in Ireland you'd have to get this Degree and that Degree and this marking and that marking in your School Leaving Certificate just to pour the tea for the other employees in a job like this! You'd probably have to know someone on the inside on top of that.' For the early 1980's Dave wasn't far off the mark! But the United States offered him something more. An opportunity to engage, to rise or fall, to excel or falter, to thrive or fade away. It was up to the individual. Nothing could stop you, only yourself. They didn't care where you were from, whether you were working-class or reared on a multi-million dollar yacht; it was who you are now. This was his personal general consensus and he was sticking to it. He was well aware of a good strong counter-argument from a European perspective but he had a life to make, had made his decision to emigrate and was set upon it.

Dave began to settle in nicely in San Francisco, made some new friends and with his weekends off, was able to explore the city to his heart's content. He mastered the Coding with flying colours and every evening, after a hectic day of Lotus 1-2-3 sheets, columns, percentages, assigning, graphs and analytical woes, he made his way home on foot through the quiet darkened streets of the Financial District and beyond to the bay. From 5:30pm the thriving city would become a ghost town. Most of the workers in the business area had long gone back to the suburbs when Dave commenced his nightly 35 minute walk around 9pm back to his apartment. He'd barely meet a soul along the way. The city centre was very quiet at night back then. It was always the same...step out onto Front St; then down and across to Vallejo St; right turn onto Battery St; straight ahead to Union St; onto Sansome St; to Chestnut St; arriving on Bay St. for the final leg down to the corner of Stockton St. and his apartment. He would mostly enjoy his walk home, the cool calm San Francisco night air upon his face. His walk appeared spooky to him at times with no one on the streets, only the occasional car and the darkness. His footsteps reverberated constantly upon the still cement as both the old and new buildings of the City stared down at him. Popping into a solitary upmarket mini-grocery store along the way, the only premises with any sign of life upon the journey; he would purchase just enough for his nightly dinner. It was nice to have someone to exchange words with each evening on his rather peculiar trip home. He thought it strange that no one other than himself and the woman behind the counter were ever there when he'd drop in. Once at home in his one-bedroom residence on the 2nd. Floor of the New Point Apartment complex he would make dinner, watch a modicum of television and often read on his little rear balcony. Such was the daily life of Dave Molloy in his new country. He was still finding his feet, enjoying his weekends outdoors and generally content. But an ominous sign of what may be on his horizon was about to occur rather rapidly; one of two omens upon his doorstep that signaled the world as we know it, is not the world as it is!

On the night of Thursday 22nd September 1983, Dave bid goodnight to his colleagues at Field Research Corporation and commenced his walk home. As he proceeded down Front St. and closed in on

Vallejo St. he felt what he would later describe as 'a presence above my head.' Looking up, he saw 5 circular lights beaming above him. They were no more than 4 yards distant from him and were directly and absolutely over him. Putting it down to the spotlights that the city often shone into the night sky back then, he ignored the situation and carried on. However, his curiosity was aroused and as he walked down Vallejo St. he looked up again. They were still there directly above his head. These were not the city spotlights! Those lights appeared far off at a diagonal distance way up in the sky. These particular lights were different. Very different. Their extreme close proximity to him, their appearance and what they were doing. Their colour was white, the same image in colour to the eye as a naked white light bulb; there were five of them, not two like the city spotlights; they were only a few feet above his head; each of them was identical in size to the other; they formed the perfect circle; they only moved when he moved; they followed him; they were moving in unison in constant steady quick anti-clockwise motion. Being vertical above him, he noticed they only moved when he did in a manner that blocked him from seeing them, for as he walked he could not see them even at a slight angle in front of him in the air. Only when he stopped and stared straight up! Dave walked further and arriving on Battery St. they were still with him. As usual, he met no one on his route. The deserted streets, the strange lights, his footsteps, the darkness. Although he was acutely aware of their presence, they made no sound. He decided to not look up while walking further down Union St. and check again when he reached Sansome St.

Stopping and arching his head back, they had remained with him. The circle they formed, the anti-clockwise movement they created, their complete and utter silence. Dave was now on edge. Nervous. He picked up his stride. He hurried past the Grocery Store with the lone lady inside. He just wanted to get home as hastily as possible from this circumstance. Onto Chestnut St. After a few yards he halted. When he stared up this time, the five lights continued rotating anti-clockwise and then came to a sudden stop! He walked. They recommenced moving with him and resumed their internal anti-clockwise motions. He stopped, they ceased their movement. He reached Bay St. He broke into a run. They kept up with him in perfect symmetry. They continued with their anti-clockwise movement and their elevation and circle above his head. In the distance Dave saw a young man, about his own age, mid-twenties, walking towards him. Twenty five minutes or so had passed since this unpleasantness had begun. Dave decided to point to the lights as he passed the fellow. Surely he would see them too. As they approached each other on the sidewalk, Dave said "Hey, you see those lights above my head?" The young man looked up but said nothing. "Well, do you see them?"

"Yeah, what the fuck is that shit?!!" came the reply. The other man looked ill at ease with the predicament. "Is that some sort of trick, those lights?" he said, as he continued to stare at them. Dave secretly hoped that maybe they'd follow that guy now. They didn't. They stayed with Dave right up to his building doorsteps at Stockton St. 'Well, they won't be able to see me now. I'll be indoors.' There were 72 apartments in Dave's complex. Most had balconies. Some faced onto Stockton St; some onto Bay St. and a few overlooked the internal gardens of the residential property. He took the indoor elevator to the second floor, walked down the carpeted corridor, turned the key in his door and threw himself onto the couch! "Phew! Oh my God. What was that?!!!" He made a cup of warm tea and calmed himself somewhat. He walked out onto his 2nd.Floor balcony overlooking the gardens. Right in front of him, facing him, eye-ball to eyeball, were five circular lights, perfectly in line with his face. They were rotating anti-clockwise. No more than three yards from him. Dave froze. They hovered there for a minute. One of them broke from the circle and shot off into the sky. It disappeared from the naked eye in seconds. The other four followed suit.

The internet's arrival was still a decade away. Its tools were unknown to the common man who would have no knowledge of its future existence. The next morning Dave awoke to a bothersome dilemma. He was uncomfortable. Troubled. He sat on the balcony in the bright Californian sunshine looking out at the airspace right in front of him where less than 12 hours before in the darkness of night a phenomenon of magnitude had occurred. 'What WERE those things? They followed me all the way home!' An encyclopedia crossed his mind. 'Maybe there'd be something in there that might explain it to me.' He stared out into the sunny Heavens and wondered. But it was more alarm than wonder. He'd have to walk home tonight. Would they be there again? Or was it an 'it?' A combination of one unit separated into five components; a U.F.O.? A Probe from a U.F.O? Had it done something to him that he was as yet unaware of? Would anyone believe him?

Having stopped in to the Holiday Inn's cozy restaurant on Sutter St. for a cheeseburger and fries before commencing work at 1pm, he crossed the Cable Car track, reminding himself to get his mind off the subject and be ready to concentrate on his Coding job upon arrival. That night walking home, he was on high alert. Every step, every dark street frightened him. He would come to sudden halts along the way and pulling his head back, look straight upwards. Nothing. On Saturday he went to San Francisco's Main Library and spent the day searching through books and some old newspaper articles. He located no specific information directly in reference to his experience. Plenty of material on Unidentified Flying Objects (even a little in the San Francisco Chronicle archives), but nothing matching five circular beams acting in unison following a person four yards or so above that person's body! On Monday he asked a co-worker to bring all works under the letter 'U' from her Encyclopedia Britannica collection into Field Research Corporation the next day. He refused to tell her why. The good lady complied but it was to no avail. Dave moved on with his life always starkly cognizant of what could transpire on his way home each night. It never happened again.

CHAPTER THREE

JANUARY, 1984.

A letter arrived from Ireland. It was from Liam Connaughton, a close friend he had grown up with back in Dublin. Liam announced that his younger brother Jim had arrived a few months before and was now living in New York City. Liam wondered if Dave was ever in the Big Apple, could he possibly check in on Jim? They had only heard from him once since he emigrated; he had never answered the phone number they had been provided; some gruff fellow at the apartment always said Jim wasn't home when they'd call and he certainly never wrote home. Jim's mother was worried and it would mean the world to the family just to get some word back. Dave put the letter down. He was well aware that Jim wasn't exactly the finest in the 'communication department.' Dave was close with Liam and the Connaughtons since childhood. 'Ah, sure it's the least I can do. A few days off anyway would suit me lovely!'

Dave waited until Sunday night when most people are home. But he tried a different tack. He rang the number Liam had given him. "Hello, can I speak to Jim Connaughton please?"

"He's not here!"

"I SAID can I speak to Jim Connaughton please!"

"Who wants to know?!"

"YOU tell him that Dave Molloy called from San Francisco and he fuckin' BETTER call me back! Did you get that, pal?" SILENCE. "Get a pen, here's my number, 1 (xxx) xxx-yyyy." Click. Two nights later just as he was getting into bed, Dave's phone rang. "Hey Dave, how are ya, how's it goin'? It's me, Jim Connaughton. How's San Francisco treatin' ya?"

"Everything's rosy over here Jim, how's things at your end?"

"Ah, good. I picked up some work at the plumbing (Jim was a plumber by trade) soon after I arrived in New York City; got me a girlfriend and generally stayin' busy."

"Well if that's the case, why don't you call your folks in Ireland and tell them?! Stay in touch with them a little more."

"Ah, I know I should. Why, did they call you or something?"

"Liam got in touch with me. They're really concerned about you Jim. By the way, what type of a character are you sharing that apartment with? What's his problem? Are you sure you are ok, there?"

"Ah, hahaha, that's Ronnie. He's from Waterford. Yeah, he's a real gem but he's grand. A decent sort, really. When I'm not working, I'm off with the girlfriend, when I'm not with her I'm with the lads in the pub. I just don't get around to remembering to call them at home. I don't mean anything by it."

"Well, I'll tell you what Jim, take a few moments to write to your mother, give Liam a call, stay in touch with them, they're all you have!" Then Dave took his idea a little further. "Liam gave me your last known address, Jim. Are you still there?"

"Yes, just the one address since I arrived."

"Ok, how about I come and visit, just for a few days, maybe a weekend with a couple of days thrown in?!"

"That would be great, Dave!" They finished up the conversation. 'Superb,' thought Dave, 'this will give me a chance to check on him in person and have a little holiday while I'm at it. See a few sights, maybe go to Carnegie Hall and take in a show or something. Aw yes, great!'

It was a sharp crisp morning in February when Dave landed at J.F.K. Airport in New York. He had taken the 'Red Eye' flight from San Francisco and although excited to be in 'The city that never sleeps' his gums were driving him insane with little bits of peanuts still firmly lodged in his orifice. 'Those damn airline peanuts do my head in, I don't know why I eat them!' Shivering with tiredness, cold and peanut issues, he wasn't one to be trifled with as he jumped in the back of the Yellow Taxi that would take him to his destination. "Woodside, Queens, please." Through the rear view mirror as they drove off, the driver eyed him carefully. "Hey Bro, you British or Somethin'? Thought I heard an accent back there. You Australian? One of them Aussies always 'Poppin' it on the Barbie,' hahahaha."

"No, I'm Irish."

"Ah, Irish, you one of the Irish Brothers, cool man, that's real cool. Hey listen, you use Irish Spring?" Dave didn't have a notion what he was talking about. "What?! Irish Spring? Like the season?"

"No, bro, you know, like the soap. Yeah, all us black brothers, we use that Irish Spring, oh man it wakes you up real good, you know what I mean?" Dave didn't know what he meant but he had some light recollection of seeing a soap labeled Irish Spring in a supermarket in San Francisco somewhere. "Well, we don't have that in Ireland."

"You don't? Ah shit, well you got Lucky Charms over there?"

"No we don't have Lucky Charms cereal over there!!!"

"Holy Shit man, we got your stuff and you don't?! You got any of our shit over there?"

"Yeah," replied Dave. "McDonald's!"

Walking down 55th. St. in Woodside, Dave searched for the house. After a short while he located it. 'Great, there it is.' Jim had taken the day off and seemed quite happy to receive him. Dave took a quick nap and they both headed into Manhattan. At the Donegal Inn on West 72nd St. they had a few drinks and a good lunch. As the conversation progressed it was clear to Dave that Jim was doing perfectly well in New York, was holding down a steady job and income and Ronnie had no hold over him in any way. Jim returned to work that Monday and Dave wrapped up his trip by doing some solo sightseeing and taking in a day excursion to the Hamptons on Long Island. At his departure he reminded Jim to stay in touch and involved with his family back home. When he returned to the Pacific Coast he phoned Liam and updated him. But New York had left a strong impression on free-spirited Dave. He had reveled in his time there. Perhaps...just perhaps. Now there's an idea!

Would Dave be the unwitting guarantor of his own personal tenet of freedom of movement? He had loved being abroad especially in the 'City by the Bay' and other than his U.F.O. experience, he relished every minute of it. His rental lease was due to expire in May. It was ideally renewable and his income was more than adequate to cover it. He thoroughly enjoyed his job at Field Research Corporation and in the relatively short time he had been in San Francisco had taken full advantage of the fruits of the city. From visits to the Palace of Fine Arts and Coit Tower, Fisherman's Wharf and Alcatraz to playing Frisbee with his workmates on the great lawns of the Marina on gorgeous summer days, his new life seemed the perfect antidote to the monotonous wet and windy days of Dublin. He had even fitted in a sojourn to the wine country of Napa and Sonoma. So why would Dave surrender his newfound stability and freedom in a city he clearly cherished to go in search of another adventure, so soon? The answer may lie in Dave's conundrum of himself. Perhaps the grass is indeed always greener on the other side. Perhaps Dave had conquered the challenge and the world was now his oyster. His strong curiosity in 'what was out there' was second to none. Or so he was finding; understanding. And it may in truth have been exactly that! Or all the prior mentioned.

The winds were changing. Dave didn't know it but his route was taking him, leading him into an odious torrent, as if unknowingly taken by a metaphysical hand and guided mischievously, menacingly, by a Machiavellian force.

LATE MAY, 1984.

"You can bunk in with me. The bed on the left is mine; you can have the other one." Dave threw his belongings down upon the blanketed mattress. There were no Box Springs or Metal Frame on either bed, just mattresses on the floor. The room was tiny. "Where does Ronnie sleep?"

"He has the room next door." They stepped back out below the naked light bulb of the living room which also doubled as a kitchen. The second floor apartment's only windows were to be found in the rear two bedrooms. Jim had cooked breakfast that morning. The leftover smell of fried liver pervaded the entire enclosure that was described as a Living Room. The musty odour had subsided but would return. A lone cockroach scuttled across the floor.

They sat down at the table. "Welcome to New York Dave, how was your flight?"

"Ah, it was great Jim, no issues."

"Listen, you can stay here as long as you like, just chip in for the rent, Ronnie doesn't care if you're here or not, I just don't understand why you didn't stay here last time, I mean you only stayed for one night really."

"Well, you know me, Jim, I march to the beat of a different drummer and besides I didn't want to intrude." On Dave's previous visit, upon their return from their day out in Manhattan, he had kipped down for the night on the lowly mattress and had awakened in the early hours to Ronnie drunkenly singing and shouting in the Living Room, causing quite a stir. Jim had confirmed to him in the morning that this was standard practice a few times a week. It didn't bother Jim, but between that and the cockroaches, Dave elected for the sake of some peace and a good night's sleep, to find himself a hotel room for the remaining three nights and to meet Jim sporadically until his departure for San Francisco. But now, he was in New York to stay and he secretly had no intention whatsoever of remaining at the apartment in Woodside, Queens. It was a good starter and that would be it. He allowed himself two weeks to find alternative accommodation.

With an excellent reference from Field Research Corporation, Dave knew precisely where he would go in search of work. There were two Political Polling/Market Research companies of note in New York City, each held in high regard in the industry. Gallup Poll and Harris Poll. He had already lined up interviews with both of them. Trained professional Coders were hard to find, so Dave hoped he would be in the driving seat at interview. The main objective however, was to secure a position. He succeeded in obtaining an offer of employment with both and selected Harris. Gallup was the most prestigious but Harris was offering him a more lucrative package. Six days after landing in the Big Apple he commenced work. He was blessed and he knew it. Now to find an apartment of his own!

CHAPTER FOUR

He decided to look in Brooklyn. He could commute on the Subway. 'I won't have to deal with walking home too far at night and that way, less chance of a U.F.O!' he thought sardonically to himself. With the New York Times Accommodation Section under his arm, he checked out a few offerings on his first two days off. He zeroed in on places close to Subway stations in better neighborhoods, his colleagues at Harris having warned him off certain unsavoury locations within the Borough of Brooklyn. He settled on Bay Ridge, an area with strong Irish, Greek and Italian-American demographics. It was here he found his home, an upstairs large apartment contained within a three-storey dwelling on 77th. St. He put down his deposits, agreed on a move-in date and returned to Woodside to inform Jim of his impending departure.

"Jaysus, you're barely here two weeks, what's the rush?"

"I need a place of my own, spread my wings, you know what I mean?! Like I said, it's just the way I am; no offence Jim and I'm very grateful to you for letting me stay here. You've given me a good start. Really, there's nothing to it other than I like to live on my own."

"No problem Dave, we were glad to have you and no offence taken." Ronnie, sitting with them, wasn't quite so considerate. A large heap of a man, his giant hairy hands laid out on the table before him; the chair beneath his rump gasping for breath and survival below all 285lbs.of him; he confronted Dave. "We're not good enough for you then?! Not up to your standards of perfection?"

"Knock it off Ronnie," declared Jim.

"No, I want to know what's his problem. You don't get off that easy Molloy." Dave said not a word. He remained silent but fixed his eyes and stare straight at Ronnie. He had previously planned to give them an extra week's rent for any inconvenience. He took the cash from his pocket and without turning or removing his stare from Ronnie, tossed the money across the table to Jim. There was a tense silence. He rose from the chair, collected his belongings and left. "Fuckin' idiot," said Dave.

Engrossed in his job at Harris, working Tuesday to Saturday, Dave made the most of his free time. He had become friends with Kevin, a UPS Delivery Driver of his own age originally from Co. Meath in Ireland, who brought parceled documents and packages on a daily basis to Harris Poll. Kevin lived in Brooklyn and so the two of them would gallivant off together every Sunday to places of interest, always dropping in for a few pints of beer in a local 'Watering-Hole.' On Saturday nights they'd go to O'Sullivan's Bar in Bay Ridge where Celtic-Rock (which was all the rage) would be provided for the packed Irish emigrant audience. Amongst over 200 people of their own age, Dave and Kevin would drink the pints, sing the ballads and play the darts amid the Saturday night mayhem. Whilst aiming for the dart board one particular weekend night, emerging from the crowd they noticed two girls, walking towards them. Jill and Sinead with their eyes firmly on the lads, took it from there. As the night progressed Dave and Jill struck up mutually satisfying delectation and soon in convivial laughter were up on the dance floor vibrating to the sounds of the Celtic Rock Shinners, a band from Dublin flown in for a few gigs in New York. Dave walked Jill home, while Kevin and Sinead bid them goodnight and headed off into the streetlights of Brooklyn, delighted with themselves.

Soon romance flourished and as the weeks passed into months and the Autumnal leaves began to fall, creating their golden carpet along the residential avenues of Bay Ridge, Dave and Jill sauntered down 77th.St. "I swear to God, if that woman tells me I'm not collating properly again, God knows what I'll do to her! She's the one who doesn't know how to collate!"

"Don't let her bother you Jill, she's probably just a frustrated old hag." They laughed. Jill worked in a Print Shop on the upper east side of Manhattan. A Co. Tipperary girl, she grew up and was raised just outside the town of Cashel, back home. They loved each other's company and were close in every way. "Between Tri Fold Brochures, Collating, demanding customers, Pop-up Displays, Custom Standard Business Cards and God knows what else, I really need a holiday, Dave."

"Sounds good, ok, maybe a weekend break down to Florida or somewhere."

"Would you?! Would we? That would be fab. Dave."

Jill lived a few blocks from Dave's place and had her rental all to herself. Paralleled by a long hallway, her living room and en-suite rear bedroom were accompanied by a small kitchen at the hallway's end. A lady of many talents and not one to boast, Dave, when first entering the apartment some months earlier had been pleasantly amazed at what he saw. An easel stood in a corner, with artist's paints and pallet strewn about the canvassed floor. Paintings she had created were loosely stacked against a wall. Books closeted on the ground between bricks with a half-empty wine glass on top, adorned the living area and her cat stood unafraid in the centre of the room, staring up at Dave. A Linguaphone Italian booklet and cassette graced a coffee table and when she asked him if he liked Lamb Chops with Mint Sauce (as she headed to the kitchen) that was it, he was hooked! 'This is a woman of fine taste,' he thought, 'and she's so funny too!' Indeed, Jill, a tall beautiful woman with shoulder-length blond hair, was sharp, nobody's fool and had a great humourous wit about her. Something Dave would be requiring in droves in the near future, as darkened clouds gathered, approaching his horizon.

On the night of the 6th.December, 1984, Jill had prepared some snacks for herself and Dave in her living room. It was 9:30pm. She closed the door behind her. Outside on the wooden-floored hallway, all was quiet. The door leading to the kitchen at hallway's end was shut. The front door of the little house was locked. Jill and Dave were leaning over a table perusing through holiday brochures, talking quietly. Dave heard footsteps upon the wooden boards out in the hall. Slow footsteps. Maybe one footstep every two seconds. Then sometimes every second. "Jesus Christ! Who's that?!!" he whispered. Jill sat straight up. There was no motion upon her face. A blank look. "Christ, Jill, who's that?" Dave stood up. He moved towards the door. The sound of each step was light but surefooted. The steps approached from the kitchen end of the hallway and were almost at the living room door. Terrified that the door was about to open, Dave reached to control the situation somewhat and swing the door open himself. "NO, DON'T DAVE, DON'T! Please don't." The footsteps passed by the door and on down the hallway towards the front door. Then a silence. Total silence. Dave looked back at Jill. Annoyed now, he swung open the door and rapidly looked up and down the hall. No one! Absolutely no one. The front door of the house remained shut and locked. Not knowing why, he checked the kitchen, the rear bedroom and adjoining bathroom. Nobody! He examined all windows and doors for forced entry. All were secure. Baffled and secretly scared he returned to Jill.

"What's going on, Jill? What was all that about? Why, well what, well, you seemed to know something about it, you told me to stop, to not open the door. Why did you do that? Who was that, or was that a.....well, I don't want to say it. Christ, Jill talk to me!"

"Ok Dave ok, oh God, how do I say this? That was Mrs. Clark!"

"WHO?!" Jill took a breath. "Alright, just listen to me, and I'll tell you about it." She took another breath. "When I rented this place I knew it was just perfect for me. I loved the neighborhood with all the little shops and cool cafes and really wanted to move in. The house was small and totally suited me. The last thing in my mind was asking anyone were there any ghosts here!" Looking back towards the door, Dave shuffled in his chair. "Go on."

"Alright well, before I met you I was in the kitchen one afternoon. I was at the stove with my back to the rest of the kitchen when I heard a chair move behind me. I turned around and the chair was no longer against the table like it had been. It was out on its own in the middle of the floor. It spooked me. I was a little afraid. Nothing else happened. I put it out of my head. I had to. I didn't know what else to do. Anyway, a week or so passed and Mr. Hernandez came to collect his rent. He asked me was everything going well and I said yeah. The thought occurred to me though that maybe I should say something to him about what happened in the kitchen. I was a bit sheepish about it, embarrassed maybe; thought he might take me for a 'silly little girl' or something, but I told him anyway!"

"What did he say?"

"What bothered me Dave was that he didn't look surprised. He just laughed and said real nonchalantly "Oh, that's Mrs. Clark. I wouldn't worry about her."

"Are you fucking kidding me?" said Dave. "Look, do you want to hear the rest of this, or not?!"

"Ok, sorry."

"He told me that the previous owner of this house was a Mrs. Clark. She was apparently a widow and lived here alone. When she died he bought the house from her son and later put it up for rent. He said I am the second tenant here and the previous renters had a few 'minor problems' is how he put it. He wouldn't tell me anymore and didn't say how he came to personally know that it was Mrs. Clark's ghost. But it fucking is!" Dave had never heard Jill curse before. She was annoyed and upset. "Have you heard those footsteps in the hallway before?"

"Yes, I did, twice. The first time I just sat in here really scared and there was no way I was going out into that hallway. The second time I plucked my courage up and opened the door while the footsteps were happening."

"Did you see her?!"

"No. Thank God I didn't see anything! So when it happened just now I just didn't want to deal with it, Dave."

"Oh, ok, I get it. Well you can't stay here Jill. This is no way to live. You can move in with me." It was late and against Dave's wishes Jill insisted on sleeping in her own bed. Dave asked her did anything like that ever happen in the bedroom? She said no. Dave hardly closed his eyes that night. Petrified that a spectre could be standing by their bed or he'd hear footsteps in the hallway, he tossed and turned throughout.

CHAPTER FIVE

Sitting on the steps of the New York Public Library on Fifth Avenue in Manhattan, Dave's thoughts wandered. It was a bright summer's day and as it always is at lunchtime, teems of people had flocked there from the offices around midtown to get a little sun and air during their break and indulge in a sandwich, a couple of hotdogs or a knish with mustard from the street vendors. Jill had moved in with him six months ago, breaking her lease and with the help of Dave, paid off Mr. Hernandez. Jill still wanted to go on that holiday and Dave was determined to make it happen soon. But unlike those sitting and chatting around him, Dave was perplexed. Bothered. The ghost of Mrs. Clark had not left his mind. That had been an unsettling and quite traumatic experience for him.

Both he and Jill could never talk about it with anyone else. 'What would people think? They'd put us down for fools.' But what really got under his craw was the fact that he had also experienced the strange lights above his head in San Francisco, following him, stalking him. 'Whether it was a probe from an alien ship or an old woman's disembodied spirit in a hallway, why did both of these entities come into MY life?' 'Why!' It wasn't that he didn't care about Jill. He knew she had suffered too at the ghostly carry-ons of whatever it was that was in that house! But why had he encountered two 'non-earthly' events of a seemingly different nature in a very personal way and within fifteen months of each other? He had lived his whole life without ever being subjected to any such things and never gave a thought to any topic in that regard. 'Just like everyone else.' But these things that had transpired were real, very real and no one would ever believe him or want to acknowledge him. He just hoped normal life stayed on track.

As the summer of 1985 advanced into Autumn, Dave continued to thrive at Harris Poll. He was well thought of and respected within the organization. He had been promoted for his analytical skills and his tracking of cultural trends. Through market research projects and contracts, he had been a key player in helping to strengthen the reputation of corporate clients, aiding them in strategic planning and prioritizing initiatives. The company had moved into Europe and had a very busy operation in London. Ireland was within their sights as another possible location. Perhaps they could tease this out by opening a Representative Office there. They had a senior management person ready to go. They needed someone with him. Someone who knew the local lingo, someone who understood the business and could handle their 'business speak' at a lower level and assist the senior man. They turned their attention to Dave Molloy. Dave wanted nothing to do with it. He was happy in New York, content in his job as it stood, settled with Jill and loved Brooklyn.

In February of 1986 he received a call from Jim. "Dave, how are you doin'? Jim here, I was just wondering how everything is goin' for ya. God, I haven't seen ya in ages, how's Bay Ridge these days?"

"All is good, Jim. Just pottering along, that's about it."

"When was I last down to see you Dave? It must be a few months now. So I was thinkin' meself and me girlfriend Ashley might drop down, say a couple of Saturday nights from now and maybe hook up with you and Jill for a night out down there in Brooklyn." Dave couldn't see why not and invited him to come on down. He'd look forward to it.

Working on a recent poll conducted on First Amendment freedoms, analyzing its data, Dave heard a familiar voice behind him. "Hey Dave, drop into my office in 15 minutes." 'What's this about?' Dave pondered quietly. 'Oh I think I know. Ah, Jaysus.' Dave waited for the invitation to sit. You don't just place yourself on a chair in Mr. Sanfey's office without the proverbial 'nod.' "Frank tells me you're not too keen on the Ireland position. Hell, it's only for a year or so Dave, maybe a few months if the venture goes tits up!" Sanfey wasn't known for his etiquette, class or societal mores. He was a direct 'no bullshit' talker. Said it like it is. A typical New Yorker in a senior position in the fast-paced world of capitalism. "Listen Molloy, what's the deal here? You're FROM Ireland, aren't you?! Surely this is a great chance to get back to the Old Country, have a few pints of that stuff you micks call Guinness and do a good job for us!" He leaned forward slowly across his desk. His voice lowered. "So, what do ya say, Dave?" "Well Mr. Sanfey, I really appreciate the offer; I'm only in my third year here in the United States and well, I wasn't really planning on a big move back home. I like it here."

"Big move back home??! Shit Dave, we're not asking you to grow old in the fuckin' place! A few months, a year, a couple of years at the most, if that. Then you can come back right here and that desk you're sittin' at will still be there. Hell, you do a good job over there and you'll be at MY fucking desk!" Dave tried to cover a quick smile. "Look Dave, you do fine work for us. Bottom line is you're a cut above the rest. We value you here. You pay us back and we'll reward you handsomely. That's the long and the short of it. The ball's in your court, Dave. Use it wisely." It was clear where this was going. Sanfey lightened up a little, cracked a couple of jokes and asked Dave to think more on it. The clock was ticking. The pressure was on.

Dave didn't want to go home to Ireland, didn't like the way things were moving. He'd resist. But he'd have to update Jill. He felt a duty to her. Keep her in the loop. When he explained to Jill the background to all this; how the company was setting up a Representative Office in Dublin; why the firm felt he was the right person to assist the senior man over there; how today the company had upped the issue with him and that although he really was not interested in going, how would it affect his tenure there if he refused; she clearly wasn't happy. "I'm not going with you, you know that?!"

"I understand Jill where you're coming from but if I have to go, I want you with me."

"No way Dave, I'm not going back there, at least not until I'm a lot older. I want to make America worth my while."

"It's only for a few months, maybe a year."

"I said no way Dave. I don't want you to leave but if you go, you can forget about us. You know what will happen. We'll just drift and next thing I know I'll hear from a friend of a friend that you're engaged to some girl back home or something." He was in a spot. "That's not going to happen!"

"You can say what you want Dave, but I'm not going with you." No more was said about it. But a caveat had entered their union and as in such cases, would complicate their relationship.

"Another drink, lads?" O'Sullivan's Bar was beginning to fill; people over in the restaurant section enjoying a meal in anticipation of the coming night's festivities. Getting fuelled up with a nice Steak and Baked Potato before a night's drinking and merriment. "A white wine spritzer, Bacardi and coke and two pints of Carlsberg." Dave returned to the table with the drinks. They had brought Kevin and Sinead along and were awaiting the arrival of Jim and Ashley. Around 7pm in they walked and coming in behind them...Ronnie! "Ah Jaysus, what did they bring him along for?!!"

"Who's that?" said Kevin.

"I'll tell you later," Dave said, quietly. They settled in around the table with the others. Three couples and Ronnie. As the evening progressed, Ronnie's loud and boisterous behaviour and smut jokes so early in the proceedings wasn't sitting well with the group. Even Jim was ill at ease. The girls tried to ignore him and spoke among each other. When Jim entered the bathrooms Dave made sure to follow. "What the fuck were you thinking bringing him along; he's a fucking asshole, listen to him out there, talking shite!"

"I had not much of a choice Dave, he kind of intimidated his way here, insisting on comin' along, ah he's not the worst, he'll probably wander off drunk at some stage."

"Well Jim, keep that big oaf away from me or I won't be responsible for what I'll do!"

By 10pm the band was playing and the establishment was thronged. Dave, Jill, Jim and Ashley were up on the dance floor. Back at the table Kevin and Sinead were stuck with Ronnie, who at this point was well oiled and restless. Kevin's home county in Ireland was Meath, a well-known and talented Gaelic football county. Ronnie's county was Waterford, where Gaelic Hurling was the main pastime and an intrinsic part of the people's lives. "You lot down in Waterford ever play Gaelic Football, Ronnie?! Not up for it, eh?" Kevin was just clowning around. He was a man of good humour with a lively spirit. He meant no harm, just keeping the conversation going in his own inimitable way. "Fuck off," said Ronnie, "you Meath bastards wouldn't know what a hurl is!"

"Take it easy Ronnie, I'm just riling you up, that's all."

"Go fuck yourself Kevin or whatever your name is!" Way over the top. Kevin immediately took Sinead by the hand and went up on the dance floor. Ronnie suddenly appeared. He, in his bad-tempered narrow–minded thinking felt he had been slighted, not once, but twice. His County had been insulted and so had he. He'd been left sitting there on his own. His childish mind exploded. He grabbed Sinead violently away from Kevin and forced her to dance with him. Kevin managed to grab Ronnie and put him in a headlock. Kevin dragged him out the back door of the premises to the laneway. There a fight ensued. Dave ran after them. When Dave reached the back door he saw that Kevin was in trouble. Ronnie was on top of him, punching him. Dave had enough of Ronnie. He ran to Kevin's aid and between the two of them they taught Ronnie a violent lesson he would not forget. When they turned to go back in, Dave noticed Jill at the door, staring at him.

Sunday morning was not the usual in their domain. Jill took her bowl of cornflakes and threw herself on the armchair. "Are we not frying up some bacon, sausage and eggs like we always do on a Sunday morning, Jill?"

"Make your own eggs Dave!" He had hoped and prayed she wouldn't carry over her anger from last night into this day. The situation was not good. "Jill, I was just helping Kevin out. That Ronnie guy was out of control all night!" Jill grimaced. "I have never seen you behave like that. It was awful to watch. Don't ever, ever, ever let me see that again. As a matter of fact I probably won't see it again as you're off to Ireland, are you not Mr.?" He realized he might be on a futile exercise here to try and redeem the state of affairs. He tried nevertheless. But it was in vain. That afternoon, Jill departed the apartment and went for a walk alone. Dave cursed Ronnie and he cursed his job. The way he saw it none of this was his fault and he hadn't created any of it. But he also understood Jill's hurt and sorrow. He wished to God he could alleviate it. When Jill returned she said she had been doing some thinking. She wanted a break. She was going to move in for a while with Sinead. She said she was confused with where everything stood. Dave's heart sunk. He pleaded with her. She was adamant.

She said she would talk with Sinead tomorrow and try to settle it as quickly as possible.

Dave's present life was going south down the tubes. Two weeks had passed and Jill seemed to be isolating him. He had only talked with her once on the phone. The rest of the time she wouldn't take his calls. She seemed to be indicating she wanted no contact for an indefinite duration. But how long would that be? 'Two more weeks? Two months? Never?' Dave had no idea. Harris Poll was getting impatient. They demanded a prompt answer now! Confused, heartbroken in his personal life and perhaps intimidated by his bosses, he said..."Yes!"

The dye had been cast. The Rubicon crossed. Ahead lay a daunting task. One which was important to the company and in which he would have to succeed. Harris began to mold him for his role in Ireland, stressing what they expected of him; preparing him for his assignment. He would leave in late April. His heart wasn't in it but that would have to change. It was imperative. As the days counted down, he reached out to Jill. Perhaps he just wanted to say goodbye and that he was sorry. That circumstances beyond both of their control had spiraled and taken a direction that had no logic. Not for them as a couple. That he actually loved her but was now caught up in a kaleidoscope of momentum that had no turning back. But when Jill heard that he was definitely going to Ireland, she turned her head and with a mournful heart, never looked back. Heartbroken at the permanent loss of Jill and the inanity of it all, both he and Jill were the unfortunate victims of the perfect.... Greek Tragedy.

Dave began to pack. The company would keep up the rental payments on his apartment until his return. He bade goodbye to his friends. He was leaving behind almost three years of life in America; a topsy-turvy endeavour of splendid achievements, tough decisions, great joys and experiences, heartbreak and unnatural phenomena. Little did he know, unaware of what was ahead, but those non-earthly occurrences he had been witness to and horrified by, were just an introduction, an icebreaker if you will, to what lay in store for him. For the telling of this true tale unfolds comprehensively with his return to his homeland and the terrible, nefarious and malevolent forces that await his arrival at a destination known as 189 St. Bonaventure Road.

CHAPTER SIX

APRIL, 1986.

Soaring through the night sky, her engines roaring, a bright Atlantic moon above her head, American Airlines Flight #6135 was on course for Dublin. Within, in Business Class sat Dave Molloy. As many Irish Newspapers as he could muster from the Air Hostess in his lap and on his tray, he intended to familiarize his mind with Irish daily life as much as he could before landing. 'My mind has been in such a different world, a different way of life, a different way of thinking for so long,' thought Dave. 'If they could only see me now back in Coolock, traveling in style via Business Class compliments of an American company.' He smiled. 'They probably wouldn't care. They'd probably say it's great to see you back and ask you little or nothing. That's the way most of them are and fair play to them. They just get on with it.' Behind him lay Brooklyn, Diners, the unity of the young Irish emigrants in the pubs looking out for each other and passing on tips about jobs, accommodation and fun places to go; the bonding. Memories of San Francisco at Pier 39, the Marina, the Golden Gate Bridge and Sausalito across the bay. And Jill. How she wanted so very much to go on that holiday he never took her on. Jill. A tear welled in his eye.

He gathered himself. His life, for now, was straight forward and straight ahead. He took a taxi from the airport. His father stood by the door. He put his strong arms around his oldest son and embraced him. Held him tightly. Dave suddenly realized just how much he needed that but in the given moment, wasn't quite sure why. His younger sisters and brother were running out to school and were delighted to see him. He sat down with his parents. His mother made him a welcome home full Irish breakfast. God, he had missed that. He lingered on every morsel. That taste he had forgotten. That wonderful taste. As evening fell with all the family home, there was a sense of togetherness, the missing link had returned. He had brought gifts from the United States for each of his siblings and doled them out, one by one. They watched television together and engaged in lively conversation. Everyone was cheerful and Dave cherished the night immensely. His parents were encouraged by the prospect that he would be home with the family for at least a year or so. But Dave had other plans.

Having lived abroad and becoming far more independent, Dave had no intention of residing within his parent's domain. He had flown the coop and once you do, he strongly believed there was no going back, certainly not for a stay of such duration. He would be a burden upon them. It would be unfair to them and indeed to himself. He would break it to them gently.

The company had increased Dave's remuneration significantly to cover increased responsibility, expenses and rental accommodation. In advance of his arrival, they had secured the services of a Dublin real estate firm to hunt down and acquire offices appropriate to the company's specifications in an upmarket central Dublin City location. The Dublin firm targeted the vicinity of Fitzwilliam Square and environs. They identified the ideal available location for the Representative Office, on Lower Baggot St. One week prior to Dave's scheduled commencement date, a front office Receptionist/Secretary, hired by the company via an agency in Dublin, had taken occupancy and commenced preparatory work. Dave had been allowed three days leave in Ireland before beginning his duties on Baggot St. With two days of a weekend tied into that, he had time to settle in. Time to prepare his folks for his inevitable exodus, to search the 'Accommodation for Rent' columns of the evening papers, to enjoy the city of his birth with leisurely strolls through its thoroughfares, to go to the Del Rio Café on Marlborough St. for his most favourite meal of all...a simple but glorious Cheese Omelette and Chips. 'They still have the best Cheese Omelette on the planet!' To sit quietly on a midweek afternoon alone at the bar in Slattery's of Capel St. fondly remembering the great nights inside these walls with Johnny and the others. These would be his short but truly-lived halcyon days. For almost upon him now would be a workload that imperatively must end in success. Also upon him would be a tribulation of such immense magnitude, a devilish nightmare straight out of hell, which few people have ever encountered or can ever come to imagine.

MONDAY, MAY 5TH.

"Hi, good morning, my name is Carolyn." She rushed forward smartly from behind the desk and reached out her hand. "You must be Mr. Molloy."

"Hi, just call me Dave." Carolyn, a thirty-something well-spoken lady from Dublin, was the consummate professional. An attractive brunette, well-schooled in the art of business decorum and impeccably presented, had been carefully selected by her Temporary Recruitment Agency for this position. Her track record was first class. She was highly regarded, astute and possessed high quality front-end office skills and knowledge. The Irish agencies operating in the corporate world were all about impressing American enterprises, gaining and retaining their accounts. There remained some prep. work to do. Frank the senior man from New York would be arriving in a few days and everything needed to be ready and finalized. Telephone lines, a fax machine and computers were in position; Carolyn had done her homework and had the office in tip-top shape, but packages of documents still had to arrive from the States; some software had to be installed and Dave wanted a proper Copier.

He was delighted with the location. The building was of Georgian architecture with its front large window providing plenty of light into the ground floor office. The address was a prime and prestigious spot for meetings in an historic yet upscale vicinity in the heart of Dublin City. It was going to be a busy week. Dave re-familiarized himself with the area, taking a walk around the locality, checking out the shops, pubs and restaurants. He was acutely aware of how Frank, his boss, who had never been to Ireland, was more than a little fond of liquid lunches in desirable extravagant establishments and hostelries. 'The first thing he'll ask me.' As the week progressed everything fell into place. They felt they had most angles covered. They awaited Frank. Once he was up and running, Dave would be his assistant and the 'Go To' guy. He would handle intermediary issues, liaise with New York, attend meetings, develop further contacts for Frank and complete an immense amount of paperwork. Frank flew in on Friday morning, went straight to the office, connected with Dave and Carolyn, had a fabulous liquid lunch and jet lagged and weary from his overnight trip, went directly to the apartment the company had provided. Exhausted, he collapsed into bed.

MONDAY, MAY 12TH.

It was a bright sunny evening when Dave sat on a lawn chair in his parents' back garden. The evening newspaper in hand, he was perusing through the 'Flats for Rent' columns. Although it was a fairly interesting day at the office, their first formal day of business, he was relaxed. Everything had taken shape, initial contacts had been followed up and Frank was pleased it was now underway. Dave required an apartment close to the city centre and was inclined to look to the northside of town with which he was most comfortable and familiar. He had his sights on any properties in the Griffith Avenue, Marino or Clontarf areas. Having glanced at many and examined a few, his eyes caught 'Bedsit for Rent, Clontarf area, All Modern Conveniences, close to shops, public transport etc. suit one person. Tel: (01)xyxyxy.' He called the number and agreed to view it the next evening. He had already discussed his intentions with his parents and although disappointed they said it was natural and they understood, so long as he dropped in to see them on a regular basis.

An elderly lady answered the door. She took him down a long hallway with doors on either side, each one with a number on it. Straight on and up a few stairs she unlocked number 6. "This is the one," she said. It was quite small. A living/dining/bedroom area (all one room). There was a walkthrough to a kitchen behind it. Other than the walkthrough, a wall separated both rooms. "Where's the bathroom?"

"That's in the hallway," she said. "It's the door with no number on it."

"Is it a shared bathroom?"

"Yes, yourself and the other five gentlemen share it." The hallway, the stairs, the flat looked clean and very tidy. "So, is this a boarding house or something?"

"No, not at all. Everyone is a tenant. You have cooking facilities in your flat, so it's certainly not a boarding house!" she said sternly. "There is a security deposit, the rent is due once a week, payable at my residence which is door number 1 and if you want to move in, I'll need work references and if you take it and decide to leave at a later date, two weeks' notice is required."

"Can I get back to you tomorrow and let you know?"

"Yes, of course." He took another look at the flat and left.

At a little bistro on Sth. Frederick St. he sat for lunch with Carolyn. "So how did it go last night, may I ask?" "Well, I'm not sure Carolyn, it was a little unusual I guess. It's a bedsit so I wasn't surprised that the rooms weren't too numerous," he laughed. "So no problem there. The rent is satisfactory to me and it's very close to the city centre. It's one of those big old houses that some wealthy family once owned and probably resided in, but today it's rented out. The rooms of the entire house are parceled out into flats, you might say."

"Oh, I see, sounds decent enough and Clontarf is a lovely area."

"It is Carolyn, it is." He didn't want to raise the bathroom scenario. He wondered why there were solely men renting in the house. Thought it was a little odd.

'Well whatever the reason it doesn't affect me. I'll just go about my business anyway.' He popped down to the Clontarf house that night, produced his proof of employment and paid the fees.

On Saturday afternoon he received his keys and moved in. 'Finally, all settled in Dublin, professionally and personally.' Wanting a mild celebration, he headed out that night to the Yacht Bar & Restaurant on Clontarf's seafront. He was joined by Eddie and his childhood friends Caroline and Bernard. Following a good and joyous evening, Eddie dropped him off at his new address. "So, what's your flat like, can I have a look?"

"Yeah, sure you can." Once inside, Eddie had a look of disbelief on his face. His expression told the story. "Are you fucking kidding me Molloy, you couldn't swing a cat in here," he said, laughing. "Jesus Christ, Dave, you'll feel like a lion in Dublin Zoo. Going back and forth in your cage."

"Get the fuck out O'Leary, before I throw you out!" They both laughed. They opened a couple of beers, shot the breeze for a while and Eddie went off into the night. Dave felt deflated. He fell asleep.

The next morning he took a look around his flat. It took him a few seconds. 'Ok, it's small, in fact it's tiny. But it's mine.' He realized there were only two jets on the gas stove. Most have four. He had never seen one of those before. There was no microwave oven and upon inspection no sockets to plug one in. He had no windows at all. What was behind the kitchen wall if there were no windows? Someone else's flat? There was only one socket and that was beside his bed. It had a small radio plugged in. One naked light bulb hung from the ceiling in each of the two rooms. The distance between his bed and the only table was about four feet and the table had nowhere to go. It was up against the wall. There was no space in the microscopic kitchen to eat. No T.V. He'd have to unplug the radio and purchase a television only to have it on the table. 'Good God, what was I thinking? I must have been asleep when I made this decision. Why didn't I just look at it a little more and inspect it properly?' Back in the States in both cities he had been on the ball when it came to deciding on an apartment. He was annoyed with himself. 'I'm here in this flat now, I'm paid up for a week and two weeks' notice is required if I wish to terminate.' He decided to see how it goes rather than just jump ship, for now.

During the next two weeks the three-person staff at Harris Poll's Dublin office were happy. The prospect of Irish corporate clients 'down the road' was looking good. Market Research was a growing necessity in the fast-becoming global world of competitiveness and Harris was firmly placed to support clients with methodical analysis. Their experience and proficiency in the field was second to none and Frank was a master at getting the message across. Two initial meetings had proven lucrative and overall it was a great beginning thus far.

Meanwhile with no laundry facilities readily available to him, Dave was trekking up to Coolock with his clothes. He would take the opportunity to spend quality time with his sisters and brother and get a little break from his flat. He was beginning to feel trapped when he was inside his new abode and it certainly wasn't a venue for visitors! At this point he had no alternative but to search for another and proper place to live and he was 'damn sure I'm going to have a real good scrutiny of the place before I accept it.' The one plus to the flat was Clontarf. He loved the neighbourhood with its serene streets, residential tree-lined avenues, close proximity to the sea and the well-heeled trophy homes that styled its image. So Clontarf it would be. There is an old adage that says 'Every cloud has a silver lining.' But for each plus there is a minus. For each positive a negative. Behind some silver linings there can be a cloud. A pernicious, fiendish, demonic cloud was upon the precipice of Dave's world. It is now Monday 2nd. June. In this true narrative of events that occurred in Clontarf, Dublin in 1986, Dave Molloy within 24 hours is going to unintentionally commence his entry into a realm of evil, both physical and mental at 189 St. Bonaventure Road.

CHAPTER SEVEN

TUESDAY, JUNE 3RD.

The evening sun was still bright in the sky as Dave Molloy seated himself on a bench in Merrion Square Park. He opened the pages of the Evening Press newspaper to the Accommodation Available section. 'Here I go again.' He exhaled. 'This time I'll make sure I'm on a winner.' 'Two bedroom, sunny views, Drumcondra area, no, I don't want that; Studio apartment, Glasnevin, no, no, too far; Clontarf bedsit, NO WAY, no more bedsits, ah wait a minute, there's a few options!'...Ultimately revealing themselves were five possible ones within Clontarf to explore. He went to a phone box. He received answers at four of them. He set up two of those for viewing the next evening and returned home to his miserable bedsit. Leaving the office an hour early on Wednesday, he hurried to Clontarf to grab a bite to eat and headed out in search of his new abode. Being far more particular now for his natural requisites, neither of the offerings were to his satisfaction. The third rental on his list appeared intriguing. 'I'll call again to see if it's still available, hopefully no one's taken it yet.' He picked up the Receiver...

Harriet attended Higher Education in her native county of Limerick. She graduated in 1985 and with a Degree in Business Studies she relocated to the capital, Dublin. She commenced employment with an advertising firm. Harriet, a tall slim attractive young woman with long dark hair, the product of a family that frequented high society was the epitome of elegance, refined in the social graces of deportment and fashion, deeply cognizant of her standing in the world, she was self-confident, sophisticated and opinionated. She settled in Clontarf.

Lorena was born and reared in the neighbourhood of Cabra, Dublin. Upon completing her education, she attained employment at Dublin Airport as a Ground Hostess. Soft spoken yet self-assured, she enjoyed Dublin's literary scene, often to be seen at book-launchings and new artistic exhibitions; she was agreeable to house parties and good conversation, her delightful humour often unwittingly being the nucleus of a gathering; she maintained a keen interest in national politics from a left-of-centre perspective. She too, settled in Clontarf.

Michael was a Dublin bus driver and proud member of the National Bus and Rail Union. Born and bred in the city, he was stationed at Clontarf Bus Depot. A generally quiet fellow, he enjoyed a social drink a few evenings a week and was well-read on a variety of subjects from Trotsky to Alfred Lord Tennyson; from Roman Civilization to Florence Campbell's Cook Book! He had a tendency to retreat into himself at times. Wanting to be closer in proximity to his job, he moved to Clontarf.

Sheila hailed from Co. Monaghan. Raised on a turkey farm, she had a wild yet appealing disposition. Spending all her school summers assisting her family on the farm, she yearned to break free. Determined to guide herself in a new direction, she had a late vocation when she graduated in Marine Biology at Kevin St. Technical College in Dublin. She gained employment with the Government and had an office in the city. She was already in her thirties when she too moved to Clontarf.

"Hello, I'm interested in the advertisement you had in last night's Evening Press. Is it still available?"

"Yes, it is."

"Ok, when would be a good time to come and view it?"

"Tomorrow night is fine, could I have your name please?"

"My name is Dave, what time tomorrow would suit you and what's the full address, there?"

"189 St. Bonaventure Road. About 8pm."

"Alright, thank you, I'll be there then."

"Thank you Dave, see you then." He replaced the receiver. 'Seems like a nice woman.'

THURSDAY, JUNE 5TH.

The leaves of the large Sycamore trees fluttered, their branches swaying in the early summer breeze as Ireland's evening light still shone. The big trees covered the entire length of the long residential road as Dave traversed the footpath. Quietness was its hallmark as the road led him on further toward the address. The houses had a similarity; all Victorian or Edwardian, most red-bricked, tall Old World grandeur, some with skylights added to converted attics; a few naturally three-storey. Terraced except for the ones at the end; a little side entryway leading to a rear garden. This was exactly what Dave was looking for, a little bit of old world gentlemanly style. The surrounding flora enhanced its mystery, its class. Long narrow gardens with footpaths led up to doorways. Dave could hardly see the numbers on the doors, such was the distance. Eventually identifying a number and by now aware they went in sequence, he counted his way, house by house, to the gate. The blinds were drawn in the big bay window. He opened the gate, carefully shutting it behind him. Approaching up the path, he saw the number...189. He was here. 189 St. Bonaventure Road.

He pulled back the big Door Knocker. He knocked twice. He waited. A tall dark-haired slender woman opened the door. "Hi there my name is Dave, I think you were expecting me."

"Oh yes Dave, please, come on in." He stepped into the floral patterned red-carpeted long hallway, tastefully appointed, noticing the magnificent chandeliers above his head. She led him in to the front living room and directly in front of him was another female, sitting relaxed upon a settee. "Please," said the dark-haired girl, pointing to a couch immediately to his right. Dave sat down. He quickly became aware the two women were sitting directly opposite him. "My name is Harriet, this is Lorena. So you're interested in living here?"

"Yes, I am."

"What type of work do you do Dave?"

"I work for an American company here in Dublin. Basically, it's an investigative office as we try to drum up contracts here in Ireland. I've been with them for a few years."

"Oh wow," continued Harriet, "so you won't be long here in Ireland then." Dave, knowing what she was getting at, replied "I'll be here in Dublin at least a year, maybe two, these things can take a while."

'That's pretty cool man," said Lorena, finally speaking up. Unlike Harriet, she had a definitive Dublin accent and Dave thought it funny to hear her use those words. He liked her. "Well, there's four of us here, another girl and a guy; the fifth room needs to be filled," said Harriet. "Come along, I'll show you the house." She took him into the hallway and they entered the Dining Room, also off to the right. Dave was speechless. He found himself in a large stately room, lushly green carpeted with a magnificent table at its centre, adorned with periodic stately chairs. On the paneled walls were Heraldic plaques and a solid-steel medieval helmet, imposing but dignified, adorned the wall to his right. Large drapes covered the regal room's window which overlooked the rear garden. One of the panes was of Church Stained Glass. "We don't use this room much, it's more cozy in the front room." Dave felt a sense of peace here in this immediate setting. He pictured himself with a glass of red Bordeaux perusing work documents at the majestic table in this grand chamber.

At the bottom of the Hallway was the kitchen. A country-style kitchen like one would expect in a grand old well-tended farmhouse. Lots of wood, pots and pans hanging from the walls with wooden comfy-pillowed chairs against a surprisingly small circular table. Dave noted the stove was small too, but thought little of it. The Kitchen's back door led to the garden. Twilight had commenced but Dave was pleased to see a long narrow garden with an unused old tree house at its rear and little flower pots throughout. A shed with a broken door completed the outdoor vista. Harriet continued on, taking him back indoors through the hallway and up the carpeted stairs. Directly at the top facing down the stairs was a door. She opened it. "This would be your room." Dave couldn't believe it. It was huge. Quite wide and extremely long, all the way down to its window above the back garden. A bed was halfway along the elongated bedroom and a large wardrobe stood in one corner. There were ample electrical sockets. The carpet was green. Harriet saw him glancing at it and said "That shade of green is parakeet. Parakeet Green," her face rushing to exude wisdom and knowledge. Next door was the bathroom, shared by all. Dave was glad to see it clean and tidy. A few further stairs going in the opposite direction to the main stairs led to a Landing above the ground floor hallway. There were three rooms off it. “Those bedrooms are mine, Lorena’s and Sheila’s. Oh, I forgot to tell you the other two persons sharing this house are Michael and Sheila.”

“Right, does Michael sleep somewhere else?”

“In a way,” she said smiling, “Michael sleeps in the attic. It was converted into a large bedroom before we ever arrived here. He has a skylight up there, he’s happy.” They went back down to the Living Room. A spacious room with the same elegant carpet as in the hallway. A television and stereo were in a corner and shelves of books upon a wall. A coffee table and the two couches complimented the décor. The front bay window gave it all character.

“Well, what do you think, I’m sorry, I didn’t get your surname?!”

“Molloy, David Molloy.”

“So, Mr. Molloy,” Harriet said, “what do you think of our grand and beautiful domicile?” a wry smile upon her face. Before he could respond, she added “Sheila and Michael are nice; she’s lovely, always busy running somewhere and Michael is quiet but sometimes he can be engaging, can't he, Lorena?"

"Oh, he can, ah yes, Michael's a cool guy. A good man."

"Well, yes, indeed yes, I'd like to give it a go, so how does it work, does one of you own the house or..?"

"The house belongs to a lady who lives in Wicklow. We've only really seen her once and I collect the rent monthly and deposit it into a special account at the bank," said Harriet. They discussed the rental cost and the sharing of the utility bills and although the outlay was significantly higher than Dave's current bedsit rent, he was well covered to afford it. "But here's the million dollar question, do WE want Mr. Molloy to move in, Lorena?" she said, teasing Dave. Lorena, tossing back her brown tresses, said "Oh, I don't know Harriet, he seems like a mystery man but an interesting fellow nevertheless, aw, maybe we'll give him a chance. Yeah, let's give him a chance." She laughed. "I'm only joking Dave, sorry, we have a weird sense of humour here, I blame it on Harriet. She's a bad influence. As far as I'm concerned you're more than welcome."

"Yes you are indeed," added Harriet. They all agreed that Dave would move in on Saturday. As he walked down the now darkened St. Bonaventure Road, Dave thought, 'Those two beautiful women are hilarious. Where would you get it? And the house is fantastic. From what they said, the other two people living there sound okay as well. I'm looking forward to this, should be fun. The place is terrific. I'm giving that bedsit notice right away. If I take a money hit by not living there for the next two weeks, I really don't care!' As Dave walked further away on this humid evening, a cold rush of air swept over the gable at 189 St. Bonaventure Road, inexplicably.

CHAPTER EIGHT

SATURDAY, JUNE 7TH.

A glorious sunny Saturday morning was upon Dublin City as Dave jumped out of bed. He didn't know it as he was still stuck in his windowless cage. He was invigorated this morning far more so than usual. Moving day! 'Out of the shadows and into the day!' He got dressed, and being a Saturday had no weekday bathroom queue and was out and about in a jiffy. Popping into the local shop for some fresh cream doughnuts, he took a leisurely stroll along the promenade of Dublin Bay, eventually finding a little seat to indulge his morning appetite. Crumbs falling, he was soon overwhelmed by a flock of seagulls, a manic flock at that! Retreating to the safety of the houses opposite the seafront, he proceeded home and phoned his Dad. He set it up with his father to be collected around 1.30pm and delivered to his new address. He settled his affairs with the Landlady, who was quite taken aback at his sudden departure. He turned on the radio and commenced packing.

"Here it is son, I hope it all works out for you here." His father leaned forward in the driver's seat and had a good look at the front of the building. "That's a fine old structure Dave, it has great character. How's the plumbing in there, it's an old house, refined as it is?" Dave hadn't got a clue. He had noticed that with four people already there, the cleanliness of the bathroom left nothing to be desired, but the plumbing? "Oh great Dad, marvelous, in great shape!"

"Well okay, if you need anything just give us a call." Dave stepped out of the car, bags at his feet. His father drove away. Dave looked up the long pathway. Through the big bay window there seemed to be a few people moving about in the front room. He took a breath. "Right then, here goes."

A young woman unknown to him answered the door. Jazz music and conversation was audible. "Yes?

Who are you?!" she said, glancing down at Dave's bags. "I'm moving in today."

"Lorena (*shouting*), there's a guy here who says he's moving in."

"Oh yeah, haha, let him in. Hey Dave," said Lorena, coming to the door, "come on in, don't mind us, we're just having a bit of a Saturday afternoon shindig." Glass of white wine in her hand, she grabbed one of his bags and helped him inside. There were two men and two other women in the living room, chatting away. The wine was flowing, the T.V. was on, Al Jarreau smooth jazz on the Record Player. Dave noticed Harriet was one of the ladies. She glanced at him but said nothing. 'Strange,' thought Dave. A man could be seen through the Kitchen's open door. "Go on up and get settled if you like," remarked Lorena, "but come back down and mingle. Get to know everyone." Dave headed up the stairs and into his auditorium. That was the first word in his mind...his bedroom was 'a fuckin' Auditorium.' Huge! He loved it. Excited, he set to work unpacking, hanging up his street clothes, his suit, his ties, all his personal belongings. He selected an area for his books; another for his Harris documents that he often brought home to review. He took his time. Put his hands behind his head and relaxed upon the bed. His eyes fixed on the carpet. 'Parakeet Green.' He laughed to himself. 'Never heard of it but its unique, I'll give it that! Parakeet Green. Haha.'

"Hey there, Lorena."

"Well hi there Dave, grab a glass of wine, there's some bottles in the Kitchen." There were a few half-bottles of Claret. Dave saw a man sitting in the back garden, found a glass, and bottle in hand made his way out there where a few chairs had been placed. 'Let's see who this is.' "Hello there, mind if I sit down, my name is Dave, I just moved in here today."

"Howya," came the reply, I'm Michael."

"Oh yes, hello, good to meet you, Harriet and Lorena mentioned you." Michael opened a packet of Carrolls Cigarettes and offered one to Dave. "No thanks, I don't smoke."

"Neither did I when I moved here," said Michael, without adding any further comment. "Are you living here long, Michael?"

"About 9 months now."

"Harriet tells me you're living in the attic. How do you get up there? I saw no steps."

"It's one of those that has a dropdown ladder. It was already a bedroom when I got here. It's private. That's what I like. They told me you work for an American company; that you were over there for a few years. How was that? What's it like? I often thought about going over there, just for a holiday though. I'd love to see New Orleans." Dave and Michael began to chat about the United States. They were relatively at ease with each other but Dave noticed that Michael never smiled. He appeared to be quite a serious fellow, but approachable nevertheless. Dave had always taken people as he found them and respected each person's individuality and uniqueness. He had however, a short fuse for 'assholes and the bullying types.' He would give them short shrift. Michael and he appeared to get along, particularly after this, their first meeting. Michael accompanied him inside.

Lorena greeted them as they entered the living room. All were there. "Hey everyone, this is Dave. Dave is moving in here today, aren't you Dave?!" she said with a big smile upon her face. "This is my friend Cara whom you met earlier and this is Sheila and her boyfriend Cathal and his friend Tom. Of course you already met Harriet." Short meaningless happy conversations ensued, as they do at such gatherings; the wine continued to be poured, a Gaelic football match came on television with Cathal and Tom loudly ensnared within its grasp; Harriet in all her finesse eloquently rising above the T.V. mayhem and Michael sat on the couch never saying a word. It wasn't long before Cathal, Sheila and Tom were off to Co. Monaghan for the rest of the weekend. Cara soon departed and Harriet announced she was off to the Theatre with some friends she was meeting in the city centre. The house quietened down. Lorena, Dave and Michael began to collect the glasses and bottles while tidying up the living room. Michael retired for a while to his attic and Lorena was off to the Fish 'n' Chip shop for her dinner. It was 6:15pm.

Alone downstairs, Dave wandered the house. 'These rooms, they're all so radically different from each other. The farmhouse-type kitchen, the 18th. Century style Dining Room, the comfortable, opulent but modern Living Room. Interesting.' There was a closet under the stairs. He opened its door out of interest. There was a light switch and an Immersion Heater switch to turn on the Hot Water. It was in the 'Off' position. Old board games and umbrellas were scattered about and coats on hooks hung in the closet. He had brought food and Lorena had shown him 'his' side of the Fridge. He made some beans on toast and ate it at the Coffee table in the front room. Lorena came home and dined with him. She gathered the two plates and put them in the sink with the glasses from earlier. She went to the closet to turn on the hot water. "Dave, would you turn off the Immersion when not using it. It costs us all money," she said politely. "Why, is it on?"

"Yes, I'm not saying you did it but, well anyway, it's a good habit to have." 'That's funny,' Dave thought, 'that was off a half hour ago. Maybe Michael was down here.' Michael was still in the attic.

SUNDAY, JUNE 8TH.

Lorena was at the table when Dave arrived to make his breakfast. In her long blue silk nightgown and matching silk pajamas, she brought a touch of class to the 'farmer's kitchen.' "There's a pot of tea on Dave, help yourself." Lorena was full of questions as he settled down with his tea and cornflakes. "Tell me all about the States, ah do, what's it like?" When she heard he had lived in two cities, it was San Francisco she was all about. "Oh wow, brilliant, must be really cool there. Do they still have all that flower-power thing going on? Oh I would have loved that. I would have fitted right in I think. All that fight the system stuff, make love not war, pot and Indian dresses." She was full of life. "What's the Golden Gate Bridge like? I saw it in a film with Kim Novak in it. VERTIGO! Yes, that's it, Vertigo, that Hitchcock film. Oh, she was gorgeous in it. Just beautiful. And that T.V. show 'The Streets of San Francisco,' ah that was brill!" Dave couldn't keep up with her. "Yeah, fight the system and all that. I'll tell ya Dave, we could do with a little of that here. Fuck those capitalist bastards out. But nothing ever changes here. Always the same old shit, Dave. More tea?" Michael arrived. "Hey Mike baby, how's it going today?"

"Alright, Lorena" said Michael. He made an instant coffee and was gone. Back to his attic. "Harriet about?" said Dave. "No, she's probably in her room. Anyway catch you later, I'm off to do my Sunday morning Yoga, see you later Alligator."

That evening all of them, except Sheila, were present in the living room watching television. "She's usually only here Monday to Friday," said Harriet. "She likes to go back to Monaghan most weekends. Always goes straight to work from there and back here on a Monday night. Michael, did you leave the Immersion on again? I discovered it on yet again this afternoon."

"I've told you before and I've told Lorena before and I'm tired of telling you, I don't leave the Immersion on. In fact, I wasn't even near it today!"

"Well somebody did. Dave you should know that we all have to donate to the running of that. It's not cheap."

"Never went near it," said Dave. "Me neither," added Lorena. "Somebody's lying, but we'll leave it at that," said Harriet.

Dave returned after a fairly busy day in Baggot St. Monday's were now beginning to be a little hectic. Frank would have to report to New York by phone every Monday, covering the previous week's business in Dublin. He'd have Dave and Carolyn on edge getting him this report and that file and rechecking everything. Dave had an opportunity to talk with Michael alone. "What's this Immersion stuff all about? Harriet seems a little testy about it. What's been going on?"

"Don't want to talk about it really, Dave." But Dave persisted. "No offence Michael, but I'm only here two days and I'm noticing a little difficulty in the air! What's the story?" Michael took a moment. "What's been goin' on is that Harriet keeps blaming everyone else for not being responsible with the Immersion Heater. The money aspect. Says we don't turn off the switch when we don't need hot water. Puts up the bills too much and all that. The thing is, I rarely use it. I wash my own dishes with cold water and when I don't I'm damn sure I turn it off. She's not the only one who has to cough up for bills."

"What about the others?"

"Lorena says it's not her and she's not sure who it is and I don't think she cares too much one way or the other. Sheila's adamant it's not her and Harriet leaves her alone about it."

"What about Harriet herself?" said Dave.

"Oh, no fuckin' way, definitely not! She's a penny pincher."

"Well, it isn't me, I only got here," said Dave, laughing. "There's more to this than meets the eye," Michael continued.

"What do you mean?"

"Well, seen as you brought this up, I'll fuckin' tell you! Nobody's doing it. Nobody. But it's happening." Dave had a bewildered look on his face. "There's weird shite going on here, sometimes. That's not all that's goin' on."

"Like what?" said Dave.

"Like things you'll hear all of a sudden, things that don't make sense, not just at night but the day as well. It's getting worse."

"Spooky things?"

"I wouldn't say that because that's not how it feels. That's too jokey a word, too silly a word. This shite's fucking serious!" Michael saw Dave's expression. "You'll see, you'll find out!" Michael took no pleasure in saying that.

Dave got into bed. The house was quiet. The conversation earlier had him thinking about the incident in Bay Ridge and even the strange lights that night on his way home. He tried to alter his contemplations.

Picking up the newspaper he read the sports pages. He didn't want to know.

Sheila properly introduced herself to Dave on Tuesday night. A big strapping curly flaxen-haired woman of a nice disposition, she was engaging and talkative. Dave inquired about her career as a Marine Biologist. "Oh I love it, I found my niche. A lot of office studies but I prefer it so much when I'm out in the Field."

"You mean the water!"

"Haha, yes exactly, in the water and by the water. A lot of river work as well. In the sea of course too, marine organisms, microbes, that kind of thing."

"Dave wouldn't know anything about exploring deep down in the big blue sea, he's more of a political statistics, market research kind of guy, aren't you David darling?" exclaimed Lorena, a roguish grin upon her face. "I do my best for God and Country," Dave said, laughing.

"I was over there once, in New York, it was great; we were at an international Marine Biology conference. The American fellas took us around to see the sights as well. I remember going to see a fabulous Broadway show. It was 'The Man Who Came to

Dinner.' Brilliant!" Sheila retired early, Harriet flitted about and everyone was in bed by 11.30. Dave was the last one downstairs. He unplugged the television and turned off the front room lights. He couldn't help but check the Immersion switch. He opened the closet. It was off. Grand. He checked the back door. Locked. Great. As he exited the kitchen he realized it was appallingly cold in there. Very, very cold. It made no sense. It was a warm night. He closed the door. Making his way up the stairs, he heard what sounded like a chair banging off the kitchen floor. He hesitated midway up. Listened. No more sound. "Fuck it." He went to bed.

CHAPTER NINE

WEDNESDAY, JUNE 11TH.

Michael had already left the house to start his early morning shift at the Bus Depot, when Dave encountered Harriet writing a note in the front room. She was fully primped and ready to depart for her Advertising office. "I'm penning a little note here for everyone to understand that I'm fed up with this. That Immersion was on again this morning. I'm sick of it, Dave. Now, I know it's not you because this has been going on for months. Maybe everyone will get the message now because I, for one, am not paying for whoever is messing about. It's childish!" She marched by him, collected her things and left. Sheila came down, saw the note, said nothing and departed.

Dave was in the hallway opening the front door to leave when he heard Lorena, who was on 2nd. Shift at the airport that day, exclaim "Oh, for God's Sake!" He assumed she had just read the note.

Michael pulled Dave aside that evening. "Did you see the note?"

"Yeah, I read it this morning."

"Let's go out to the back garden Dave, I want to talk to ya." Michael lit up a smoke. "Are you sure you don't want one?"

"No, I told you, I don't smoke."

"Well, you'll be fuckin' needing one after I tell you some shit. I mean, she's (Harriet) taking it a bit far now. She's like a fucking child. Thinks she's the boss around here or something."

"What's on your mind, Michael?"

"I just read a book about the Roman Legions. They were led by fellas called Legates. They'd often punish their own soldiers by having them stoned to death. If they took women soldiers in their Roman Army, I guarantee ya, SHE would have had that job! She'd love it." Dave tried not to laugh. "Look Dave, we're all fed up with the Immersion talk. It's been going on way too long. You'll probably think I'm crazy but there's a presence in this house and it doesn't feel friendly. Things happen. To be honest with ya, it's unnerving, very scary at times. Especially when you're on your own here." Michael pulled hard on his cigarette. "Have you discussed this with Lorena or Sheila?" Dave inquired.

"A little bit; more so with Lorena. She knows. She's well aware of it. Told me she has had her own experiences. Seems calm enough about it though. She says there are other dimensions and we shouldn't try to hinder that type of thing."

"What about Sheila?"

"Sheila knows fuckin' well! In fact, she's terrified of it. About 3 weeks ago she screamed real loud in her bedroom one night. I came down from the attic to see what was going on. Harriet and Lorena were in the Landing asking her was she alright? It was almost daylight. She was white as a sheet. But she wouldn't tell us. Just said she got a fright in her sleep. But she wouldn't go back to bed. Stayed up and went downstairs. She still refuses to talk about it. And something else....when she heard me and Lorena talking about a presence in this house she walked out of the room. She looked petrified."

"Christ, Michael, this is some heavy duty stuff."

"Well, getting back to the Immersion, I got in one afternoon from my shift. There was no one here so I decided to take a bath. I went to turn the Immersion on and after I did, within a second or so, the switch started turning off and on right in front of my eyes. I mean literally moving right in front of me. Real fast too. It freaked me out. I mean, I thought, how is that possible?! I don't care what you think Dave, I'm telling you the truth."

"Don't you feel a bit uneasy in the attic, if what you say is true?"

"It seems removed from it all in some way. I can't explain it. Just like the Dining Room. Nothing ever happens there. But I guess I'm fooling myself, about the attic, I mean. I hope not." Dave thought about the peaceful feeling he gets in the stately Dining Room. They went back inside. Nothing more was said.

The weekend finally arrived and Dave needed a break. He had hoped to enjoy his first non-moving-in weekend in this rather grandiose house; relaxing in the garden, pottering aimlessly about. Irrespective of what he had heard during the week, he was falling in love with the house; its chandeliers, heraldic plaques, expensive carpeting, stained glass window. There was something regal about it, something majestic. But Michael's words remained to the forefront of his mind; the angry thud of the kitchen chair, the icy coldness of that room. He opted to go out for the day.

He phoned Frank. "Hey, it's Saturday, want me to show you a little piece of this country?"

"Yeah, thought you'd never ask, that would be great!" They met at Westland Row train station. "Where are we going?"

"Wexford!" Dave knew Wexford Town well. He hadn't been there for years but recalled with affinity the many holidays in the town and on the beaches with his family as a child and weekend trips there with his friends in his late teenage years. As the train rumbled south through the fields and landscape of Ireland, Frank was enamoured with the opportunity to be served alcohol on a train. Back in the States you had to go to the Drinks Carriage to get a beer. "Hey, another can of that Guinness stuff and keep it comin'!" The food and beverage man with the drinks cart got a buzz out of him. "God damn it, you guys do a great job, this is some country you got here, beautiful scenery, beautiful colleens and beautiful beer, holy moly, where would you get it?" he said gleefully. "That's stout, not beer," said Dave. "Shit, man, whatever it is, it's like a goddamn meal, shit, I guess I won't be needin' no dinner tonight." Dave was amazed by Frank, in that Frank could be hilariously like this when he was off work and a cultivated professional and shrewd businessman when he was engaged in his occupation.

Strolling through the narrow laneways and streets of ancient Wexford Town with its bustling shops and harbour, Frank asked about its history. His questions were pertinent and to the point. Dave was impressed. Wandering through Selskar St; Dave told him of the waterfront where small settlements of the Irish Gaelic people fished, washed and swam; how the Vikings came and utilizing the waterfront built the town and began the harbour of Wexford; how in 1169AD the French-speaking Normans arrived from Wales and forcibly took the town from the Vikings who had been paying taxes to the local Irish Chieftain Mc.Murrough; and how the Normans shaped and enhanced the town to what it is today. "Tell me more," said Frank, while buying a memento of Wexford to mail to his niece in America." "But tell me in a pub!"

Imbibing pints and enjoying a hearty hot meal, they saw out the afternoon, with a local drunk providing Frank a personal rendition of 'The Boys of Wexford,' a rousing song of patriotism and pride that dwells in the heart of the Irish nation. Rumbling back to Dublin upon the clickety-clack of the railway, Frank took a nap. The moving train transported Dave ahead to Clontarf.

When Dave climbed the stairs to go to bed that night, he heard humming sounds coming from Lorena's bedroom. He could see through the gap beneath the door that the light was off. He noted it wasn't a murmur to a song or music, just a low haunting hum. A hum. Candles appeared to be flickering from inside.

SUNDAY, JUNE 15TH.

As Dave approached the kitchen door he wondered why it was shut. He could hear activity in there. Then he saw the hand-written sign upon the door.

SUNDAY SPECIAL SMORGASBORD.
For Residents of 189 St. Bonaventure Rd. ONLY.
ENTER at your DELIGHT.

Charmingly amused, he entered. Lorena greeted him. Throwing her arms aloft, "Welcome darling David to the kitchen of milk and honey. For your epicurean pleasure, may I present you with a wide selection of French cheeses, Edam from Holland, Parisian Croissants, an assortment of fruit incorporating our St. Bonaventure Road repertoire of strawberries, melons and bananas, not forgetting an accompaniment of farm-fresh boiled eggs, and our collection of cereals flown in at the Management's great expense. And if you want sausage and bacon, you can make it your fucking self!" Dave broke into howls of laughter. Indeed in front of him, was an exquisite display of delectations Lorena had so engagingly introduced, spread across the table. "Thank you so much Lorena, you are a treasure." Even Michael was laughing. "Lorena does this once a month, I always make sure I'm here for this spread!"

"So, lads, where's Harriet?" said Dave. "She was here earlier, talked for a few minutes, grabbed a slice of cheese and went back upstairs. Harriet is Harriet, we take her as she is," said Lorena, casually.

It had been a while since Dave had laughed so much. He was fond of Lorena. She brought life to every room. Over breakfast, the three of them at ease with each other talked about everything and anything. Words flowing, sharing the croissants, the to and fro of good conversation…"yes I like Yoga, helps me relax, it's great for posture and concentration, a feeling of well-being."

"Not for me," said Michael, "I prefer to read. That's my mantra and I hold by it." He smiled. Dave remembered the sounds from the bedroom the night before. "I was going to bed last night and I think I heard you humming, is that some Yoga exercise?"

"Yes it is but that's not why I was doing it. I wasn't doing Yoga last night. I'll be at my Yoga later today though. Every Sunday, it's enough for me."

"Oh, ok," said Dave, somewhat confused. "Tell him why you do it, why you hum, go on, tell him Lorena. For fuck sake, I can hear you myself from the attic, hear you below me, humming away!"

"You want me to tell him, really want me to tell him, I mean, he's only here a little over a week," said

Lorena. "Sorry, I already told Dave a couple of things, so maybe there's no harm..."*interrupting...*"You told him?"

"Not too much really," came the reply. Lorena looked straight at Dave. "Well Dave, looks like the cat's out of the bag. I wanted you to enjoy your living here and if you found out, then so be it. I wasn't sure he'd bother you."

"Who?"

"Let me make more tea and we'll talk." She put the kettle on. Michael settled into his chair. He seemed relieved that Dave would be privy to more information. "Are you an opened-minded guy, Dave? My instincts told me you might be. I'm not asking you to accept, just to be open-minded, objective not subjective; Michael and me and Harriet and to an extent Sheila are an unusual group I guess; we accept. Well, maybe not Sheila, that's why she goes up to Monaghan on weekends, she's very scared, she's only here when she has to be, but she accepts." Dave was quiet. "Harriet was here first, maybe that's why she likes to think she's in charge (*she laughed),* then Sheila, then Brian, then Michael, then little ol' me."

"Brian, who's Brian?" said Dave. "Oh, I forgot; you took Brian's place!" she said pleasantly. She went on..."There were no incidents or anything like that in this house for a long time; that's what Harriet told me. You know, normal life. About 6 weeks after I got here strange funny little things occurred. Sometimes when we were all together in one room, sometimes alone, both day and night."

"Like what?" Dave said. "It started with the back door here in the kitchen slamming. We all heard it. We were in the living room. We thought someone had broken in because it wasn't locked and they banged the door for some reason. Brian and Michael checked the house. There was no one. It happened twice more that same night. It banged so hard, like on purpose. We finally locked it, belatedly I'll admit. That was it that night." "Was it windy out?" "No Dave, nothing like that. Anyway, Sheila was in the kitchen just before going to work a few days later and she said someone or something pushed her in the back. Heavily. She said she fell forward. She described it as the feel of a person's hand pushing her angrily."

Michael interjected. "The day after that happened to Sheila I was walking down the footpath in the front garden on my way to work. It was half-four in the morning because I was to drive the early bus out of Clontarf Depot. It was still very dark. As I walked down the garden footpath I got tripped. When I say tripped I don't mean tripping or falling over something on the ground. I mean it was like a leg put out in front of me. It was across the middle of my shin! I mean that, the middle of my shin!" Lorena continued..."Whoever's last up to bed unplugs everything. That's the generally-accepted rule. What began to happen regularly was that no matter who did the unplugging and turning off of lights, whoever was first down in the morning would find everything plugged in, the T.V. on and all lights on!" Michael added, "It was usually Harriet or me who was down first and it still is. So we can both attest to that. Sheila is down first occasionally and she comes upon the same problem. The doors are always still locked, as they should be. Harriet used to think that one of us was messing, either Brian or me. But as more and more happened and as things have increased, she accepts that's not the case. However, the Immersion is different, she won't bend on that. It's like she wants to find a normal reason for one of the problems. Anyway, she's too much of a skinflint."

"Then about three weeks ago, Harriet was white as a sheet," said Lorena. "I found her on the couch just looking into space. That's not like her! When I asked her what was wrong, she told me something awful had upset her in the kitchen. I asked her about it and she said "*I'm not going to talk about it, ever!*" In short, Dave, and there is more, we have heard a thumping on the bannisters at night; Sheila's bedroom door has been pounded on, Michael has seen the Immersion switch moving by itself, I have heard footsteps in the Landing frequently and I am not afraid to go out and check and there's never anyone...no one in the bathroom, just no one and yes, the lights do be on downstairs and when I go down to have a look around, nobody. I then turn them off. A couple of hours later, they find them on again and everything plugged in again. We've also had the television channels change right in front of our eyes with no one doing it! Harriet said she was in the backyard shed the day before you arrived here and as she was leaving, absolutely everything on the shelves came down violently on the ground, fucking simultaneously!"

"Okay folks, hold on a minute," said Dave. He was not in good form anymore and he had questions. Given his two recent experiences, albeit minor ones in comparison, he felt like he had been thrown from the frying pan into the fire. "Who owns this house? I know it's a woman in Wicklow, but who exactly?"

"Don't know for sure, like I said Harriet was here first, she collects all our rents and I suppose Harriet represents us," replied Lorena. "Was Harriet here by herself until everyone started coming in, one by one?"

"Yes." Dave pondered. "So that tells us no one was here immediately before Harriet; that there was a gap between her arrival and the previous occupants, whether owners or renters."

"Yes."

"So, what we have to find out is, why did they all leave? Was it a sale to a new owner who immediately leased it out; or did that owner take occupancy and then change her mind for some unknown reason; or were there tenants here, four or five of them who all hightailed it at the same time? If so, why? Did the owner have to start again fresh with new tenants, specifically us?! I would ordinarily suspect that some wacko has keys to this house and the lunatic is sneaking in here at night and having fun but I have to admit that's preposterous. The shed incident and the behavior of the television rules that out, along with a few other things you mentioned."

"Listen to me, Mr. Detective, we know better than you what's going on here, we've experienced it first hand and to tell you the truth it's frightening; don't tell me what I did or didn't experience out on that garden path or Lorena, Sheila or Harriet. What do you think...that we are all fuckin' liars?!" said Michael furiously. "Why did Brian leave?" said Dave. "I'll give you one guess," said Lorena. "It got too much for him. He said it was going to increase. He was always afraid going to bed. He would hear footsteps on the Landing too and his bedroom door was pushed wide open in the early hours. He saw no one but that was Brian's last straw. He literally left us that same day." 'Oh Jesus, that's now my bedroom,' was the first thought across Dave's mind. Lorena and Michael added that between four and five in the morning is the most active time for the unpleasantness.

"Lorena, you said you weren't sure if he'd bother me. What makes you be so sure this thing is a man?"

"He's a sad and angry man, Dave. A big fellow too. I try to make contact with him if I'm in the mood. To help him move on to where he's supposed to go."

"WHAT?"

"I've seen a towering black enormous shadow in my room. Sheila has too. Once anyway. I do talk peacefully with him, to try to encourage him to pass. The humming is part of that."

"What do you mean?"

"It's hard to elaborate to you, Dave. If you were there you'd understand. You'd get it." Dave turned to Michael. "Why don't you all just leave here?" Lorena quickly answered for him and for herself and Harriet.

"There is something beautiful about this house. Almost enchanting. It has elegance, character. Let's face it, it's not like anywhere any of us have ever lived or more than likely ever will. It draws you in, keeps you. Wraps you in its arms." Dave knew exactly what she meant; he was smitten with its charm and grandeur. "Sheila is a little uneasy, we don't know if she can hack it, but we'd like you to stay. He's not going to hurt anyone. He's reaching out and he's angry. He must have lived here once. I think he's trapped or perhaps he doesn't want to leave."

'How can this transpire? A development in my life I do not want. I cannot believe that first I am harassed by objects flying right above me and then zooming off into thin air. The footsteps that night with Jill horrified me. Mrs. Clark, wandering her home. Nothing untoward in my life until those two events. Suddenly I have this to contend with. Oh God. I'm tired of moving, so tired. I love this house. I like everyone here, even Harriet in all her vain glorious mannerisms. Her prim and proper pretentiousness. Yes, even her. I didn't want to tell them about the chair banging in the kitchen. I wonder why? Am I too self-protective? Or just a fool. I pray to the Holy Spirit and to the Lord Jesus Christ to protect us all in this house. Oh, I'm tired. So very tired. I miss Jill. I miss her so much.' His head sunk deeper into the pillow, his eyes closed with sleep.

View from Dave's bedroom door

CHAPTER TEN

TUESDAY, JUNE 17TH.

"I'm going to entertain all of you this evening, although I have no idea why I'd want to be a mammy to the likes of you lot!" They had no idea what Harriet was talking about. "Really, what's going on?" said Sheila. 'I'm making you all dinner. We'll have a soiree, no less. You can select the vegetables, we'll have our usual wine and of course, my superb main dish! I think Michael is the only one who has eaten already, so... and I'm sure Michael will be well able for another go at dinner. So nobody cook and Lorena and Sheila, you can help me in the kitchen."

"Harriet's making dinner! And for all of us? This has got to be a first! Harriet, ma cherie, what has come over you? We, a simple ragtag bunch of peasants and delightful Harriet shall feed us. Pray, tell us, speak!"

"Oh Lorena, knock it off unless you wish to starve."

"What's the main dish, Harriet?" asked Sheila. "Osso Buco."

"What's that?" said Dave. "Oh, my poor Dave, you have no idea, do you? You have been too long in America stuffing yourself with hamburgers and ketchup! Please, a little class. Osso Buco, for the benefit of you and our fellow diners is Veal Shanks, white wine, carrots, olive oil and fennel. But we require more veggies, so that's up to the girls!"

"What's up with her?" whispered Michael to Dave. "Is she on some magic pills? Fuck me, this is a surprise!"

The door remained open in the kitchen as the three women set about their task. Happy talk, giggling and wine sipping continued throughout the aromatic proceedings but for the most part neither Sheila nor Harriet were left alone there, not even for a second. Lorena stayed by their side. Except while setting the grand table in the oft' unused Dining Room, she mentioned to Dave that he'd have to do the rest of the setting, as Harriet and Sheila were uncomfortable in the kitchen without her there. 'God, this ghost thing is dramatically affecting this household,' thought Dave. All had been quiet on Monday and the plugs and electric had not been interfered with either then or Tuesday morning.

An enjoyable feast was had by all with everyone entirely relaxed in the Dining Room. Michael recited a poem by Patrick Kavanagh while Lorena entertained with *'Chanson D'Amour!'* As the soiree was nearing a conclusion, the T.V. suddenly came on in the adjoining Living Room; a loud burst of volume, the decibels rising and intense. Blaring! Everyone froze. Dave plucked up his courage and went in. Harriet followed. The room was empty. Dave turned off and unplugged the television. He went to the hall. The front door was locked. He angrily marched into the kitchen. The back door was locked too. As he exited, he heard footsteps, heavy ones, on the Landing upstairs. So did the others. Lorena and Dave went up. The footsteps had ceased. All clear visually. All the bedrooms clear. While briefly checking Lorena's bedroom in her presence, he saw candles and stones in a circle on the floor. A fairly wide circle. He asked her about it. "Ah, that's just me. Nothing to worry about," she said. They returned downstairs. 'I'm sleeping in your room tonight, Harriet," said Sheila. Michael was quiet but very uneasy. Not long after, they all went upstairs together at the same time. On the Landing, they talked with each other. 'It seemed psychologically to help,' Dave would later write in his diary. Harriet reminded everyone that there were five of them; that if anyone wanted they should just come to another room like Sheila was already doing, and bunk up. "Except the men should stick together," she brazenly laughed.

It was on this night that Dave Molloy decided to begin a diary. A diary of events thus far and of anything that would unfold. He had tonight discovered that fear can turn to anger, to a stubbornness against evil which is ingrained in every man. Only a few utilize it. Only a few know they have this gift within them. They learn from the great tutor that is fear. He was fully cognizant that the dread would return to every bone in his body. Yet tonight he had risen above it; something inside a human's soul that says "Don't toy with me like this. Do not instill fear in me. I have every right to be here, you do not!" Dave Molloy didn't fully grasp it but he was not the customary man. And it is this that would propel him to tell a story. A remarkable story. A true story emerging from and documented in his diary. A diary that relates the awful events that occurred and were witnessed by five young people in a house in 1986, in Clontarf, Dublin.

Wednesday, June 18th.

'Lights on again, all electrics plugged in.' A simple morning note written by Harriet and left for the others to see. Dave took the bus into the city centre and making his way up Lower Fitzwilliam St. his mind wandered. Roamed from electrics to analytics; from doors slamming to the Welcome Mat at his office on Lower Baggott St. He would have to concentrate on his work at hand today. He had a job to perform. His concentration levels on behalf of Harris that morning were at best, passable. The afternoon brought an improvement as the business of the day swept him along.

No one had much to say in the living room that evening. The episode of the night before delivered an unsettled, almost embarrassing feeling within the collective. Assembled together in the room no spontaneous offering of dialogue emerged. Michael was now far more comfortable amongst his fellow dwellers than remaining by himself alone up there in the attic. He quietly read a book. Sheila sat close to Harriet. Lorena ironed her uniform while Dave sat at the edge of the couch munching on some crisps. The T.V. channel changed! The remote was on the coffee table untouched. The channel changed again! Then quickly again. Everyone stood up. The television channels then rapidly, extremely rapidly, at a speed faster than a change per second, kept interchanging. Dave whisked his eyes to the remote. "JESUS LORD GOD!" Harriet rushed over. "Oh my God." They all stood around the remote on the coffee table. Their mouths dropped! The buttons on the remote were being compressed. Not by any of THEM! The compressions were at an incredible velocity. The televisions' actions were so accelerated that no channel could be witnessed for even half a second. Essentially, it was just a massive haze of speed. The remote compressions kept up. Then stopped.

Sheila and Michael were visibly upset. They had not observed compressions on the remote last time. Harriet appeared dazed yet retained her protocol. But Lorena and Dave were a different story. Lorena was ebullient. Her excitement elevated to something bordering on happiness. "This is unbelievable stuff. Wowee, we're actually experiencing this. Think about it, who gets to see such wondrous things? We've got to really take it all in. He's so cool."

"You've lost your fucking mind!" yelled Sheila.

"Whoever 'he' fucking is, this son of a bitch is not getting rid of me!" Dave angrily said. He was livid. He turned to the room itself and looking up and around he roared "Fuck you, you bastard! You think you can get rid of us? This is OUR house. WE live here. Not YOU. You have no right to be here. You have no right to interfere! FUCK YOU, I'm not budging. Go fuck yourself!" Everyone was silent. Harriet looked at him admirably. Lorena had a big smile upon her face. "I can't take this anymore," said Sheila. "I'm getting out of here." No one spoke. How could they? Michael just said "Oh Christ, I don't know about all this, I just don't know," and put his head down.

They disconnected the television and stayed together in the room. When Michael said he wanted a drink he unashamedly asked Dave to go to the kitchen with him. "Let's have a séance!"

"Lorena, are you referring to where a group of people all gather round a table joining hands and calling on spirits like they did in Victorian England?" said Harriet. "Yes, exactly."

"That is so dated. That's all nonsense. Really, Lorena, I know you're an exuberant girl but get with the programme."

"No, no, we might be able to help him. To get to the bottom of this. If he's as spiritually strong as he is showing us now then he'll definitely come in response to us at a table. But we all need to do it together. It's probably no good if there's only one or two of us. No point."

"Well I want nothing to do with it," Sheila said emphatically. "Me neither," said Michael. "Oh come on all of you, don't you want to solve this? He needs to move into the next life, in another dimension. He's stuck here trapped in this house and he's angry."

"Oh, is he? I hadn't noticed," said Dave. "I'll tell you what though, I don't give a fuck about HIM but if there's something to it, if it brings peace to this house and all of us, maybe. But it might make things even worse, Lorena."

"There's a psychic group in England that can help. They do séances and take charge of the situation with the affected people sitting with them at a table. They're professionals at it. They could help us."

"How do you know about them, Lorena?" asked Dave. "They cleansed a house in Cabra, there was an article about them in the Sunday paper. They came over here to Dublin to help a family. Well, they didn't actually 'clean the house' as it's called, but they were able to tell them information and help them. Apparently they have had successes in the past, though." Harriet spoke up. "Something to consider perhaps, but how would we contact them?"

"I have their number!" I got their name from the paper and I got their number from the Irish Telephone Exchange, basically they just got the number from the English telephone directory. So, will we give it a try?"

"Hold your horses," said Dave, "let's think about it."

"Harriet. Will you do it?" Lorena said. "Yes, okay."

"How about you Michael?"

"I suppose it's worth a try."

"Sheila?"

"No!"

"Dave?"

"I will. I'm a bit disturbed about this, that it will ignite the situation further but, I will."

"Ok, so there's four of us. Sheila, you can just sit out the proceedings, maybe wait in the Dining Room, nothing ever happens in there."

"I won't be waiting anywhere!" I won't even be here for that. This whole thing is crazy, everything that's happening in this house. You're all bonkers, for God's sake. We should all just leave. Harriet, can I sleep in your room?"

"I think it's not suitable, why don't I move in with you Sheila, your room is much bigger. My box room is just a little too small for two of us. We can't really do that again."

Dave decided that from now on he was leaving the light on in his room at night. He had also bought a flashlight for fear that the entity would knock off the lights. 'If he's capable of turning on lights, he's capable of turning them off!' At 4.50am a terrible banging was heard somewhere near the base of the stairs. Everyone except Sheila went to investigate. It seemed to be a thumping on the bannister. It continued for a few moments as they watched. It was violent. It stopped.

Sleep was being interrupted. But they were of an age that in the main, they were clearly coping. Lorena phoned Dave at his work. "I called the psychic group in England. They asked me a lot of questions. They took up my whole break. Anyway, they said they would discuss it and get back to us."

"When?"

"They said in a few days."

As he hung up the phone, Carolyn said "Mr. Kelly rang us again. He wants to set up a meeting with you and Frank."

"Why the fuck didn't you go ahead and just set it up, Carolyn, for fuck sake!" raising his voice. She was aghast. "Oh my God, I'm so sorry Carolyn, I'm so sorry. I have things on my mind. I hope you'll forgive me. I'm so sorry." He was disgusted with himself. He felt terrible for Carolyn. The pressure of the house was beginning to build, creeping into his everyday psyche, into his place of employment. 'Was this happening with the others?' he wondered.

That evening Sheila announced that she was actively looking for another place to live. Harriet tried to reason with her but eventually admitted that reasoning was a redundant activity in this case. "Sheila, it'll be alright, there's no need to go," said Lorena, realizing that maybe there was! Even Lorena understood the stress Sheila was experiencing. Sheila was immoveable. "Where will you go?" asked Lorena.

"As far away from Clontarf as I can get!" came the reply. "But it's such a gorgeous area. Would you not stay local so we can stay in touch a little bit?"

"Absolutely not, Lorena! In fact I'm going to move to the southside, maybe Ranelagh or Sandymount or somewhere. Miles from here if I can help it."

Dave asked Harriet to get in contact with the owner. Talk to her about the house. How old is it? Had she rented it to other tenants in the past? Had she lived in the house herself? Most of all, was she aware of unusual occurrences in the house? In fact, did she damn well know there was a violent presence in the house?!!! If she did, why wasn't anyone here told? Harriet agreed. "She'd never admit though," said Harriet. "She's making money on this house. Why would she admit it, if she does know?"

"It doesn't matter, Harriet. Give her a call. Ask her to come here and we'll talk with her."

"Okay, I agree. I'll give her a buzz."

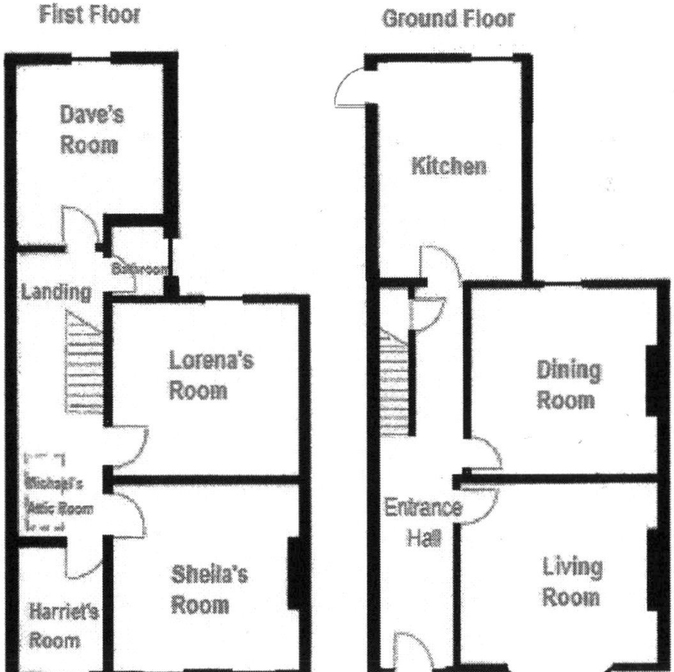

First Floor
Dave's Room
Landing
Lorena's Room
Michael's Attic Room
Harriet's Room
Sheila's Room
Ground Floor
Kitchen
Dining Room
Entrance Hall
Living Room

CHAPTER ELEVEN

FRIDAY, JUNE 20TH.

On the evening of the 20th.June, Harriet informed everyone but Sheila (who had gone straight to Co. Monaghan for the weekend after work that evening) that she had phoned the owner. "What did she say?" Dave inquired.

"She wanted to know why we needed to meet her. I told her we needed to meet in person and that I'd discuss our concerns with her then. But she refused to come to the house. So, I said alright then, can I meet you for lunch in the city centre? But she said "when you are depositing the monthly rent next Friday I'll meet you outside the bank." I thought that was a bit much, but she was determined. She clearly won't meet us here; she won't even sit down with me in a café or restaurant."

"She knows something," said Dave.

"Yes, she may, anyhow I agreed to that, for now. I think we all might need a break. Michael, you love to read and consequently I think you might like the theatre. Lorena and Sheila do. What about you, Dave?"

"Yes, I might like the theatre. Why, what's on?"

"*SIVE*, by John B. Keane is on at the Abbey."

"What's that specifically about?"

"It's about a young girl coming of age who through a local matchmaker is being forced to marry an old man against her will. Her aunt and uncle stand to make money from the match. But Sive, that's the girl's name, is in love with a fellow close to her own age and so she's in a predicament. Plus, there's a further intricacy to the story. It's set in Co. Kerry, I believe."

"Oh yes, *SIVE* is a great play," said Lorena.

"So, you want us all to go to a play together," Dave said. "Yes, I actually do, Dave," said Harriet, a commanding authority about her. "It would do us all good to get away together from here one night. I inquired and there are tickets available for next Thursday night's performance. I think we all could do with a badly-needed respite."

"Superb," Lorena chimed in, "and we can go to a restaurant for dinner beforehand, direct from work. No need to come here first."

"Where to?" said Michael.

"How about Gallagher's in Abbey St?" Lorena loved Gallagher's. It was settled. Harriet would buy the tickets, collect the money from the rest and they would rendezvous at Gallagher's.

As the night progressed, the lights in the living room continuously flickered. Non-stop. Then the kitchen lights faltered likewise. Just for the hell of it, Michael and Dave checked the Breaker Box. The kitchen and front room were not on the same breaker and all breakers appeared fine. Lorena went up to her bedroom about 10.15pm. Later, Dave ran up the stairs to use the toilet. As he emerged from the bathroom, he noticed Lorena's door ajar. He knocked. She invited him in. "I came in to ask (*midsentence, he was stunned)*...Good Jaysus!" Before him, his eyes befell Lorena, sitting cross-legged on the carpet, at the perimeter of a circle she had set up on the ground before her. The circle was of perfect symmetry, made of little rocks and lit candles. The diameter was wide, creating a big circumference. The main light in her room was switched off; a small lamplight lit in a corner. The flickering light made everything surreal. Against the wall was an acoustic guitar he had never heard her play. Salvador Dali works displayed themselves throughout this, her private space. "What are you doing?"

"This shouldn't be a surprise to you Dave, you saw my room quickly the other night when we heard the footsteps up here on the Landing. You even asked me about it."

"Yeah, and I've wondered about that since. But Lorena this is even more. I mean, it's all so" *interrupts,* "Bizzare?!" she said annoyingly "No, not the Dali paintings,' said Dave, "but what is this circle, WHAT is all this?"

"I'm communicating with him, creating an aura, a pleasant environment for him to enter, without ill-will and all that ignorant mind-blowing crap. I read about it years ago, how a circle is open to all, a kind of portal for the spirit world to enter without fear or judgment."

"Do you realize what you're doing, you're ATTRACTING HIM IN!"

"No I'm NOT! He was here before I even arrived in this house. Harriet told me. So did Michael and Brian! In fact, he's probably been here for years, probably even before our Grandparents were born! But he's a prisoner in his own house and he can't get out. I'm trying to get him to realize he has to proceed to the next higher dimension or wherever!"

"Prisoner in his own house? Well he can certainly get to the back garden after what Harriet told us and Michael told us about being tripped on the front path."

"I mean on the property itself for God's sake! Dave, I don't think you fully understand or even want to."

"Well if he is here years, I'm going to the nearest Library and see what I can dig up."

"You do that Dave!"

Throughout that night a door banged furiously, over and over. Harriet knocked on Dave's bedroom door and asked him to accompany her downstairs. When they went down they witnessed the door to the kitchen slamming shut and opening incessantly.

SATURDAY, JUNE 21ST.

Dave went to the library that morning. He struggled to locate information. After a couple of hours he departed and phoned his friend Liam (Jim's older brother). He needed a few drinks. Liam picked him up at the house in Clontarf. Dave made sure to wait for him at the gate. He didn't want anything happening indoors in Liam's presence. Too much to explain. 'How do you explain to someone who isn't experiencing it day by day?!' Dave couldn't deal with that right now. The very reason he wanted a drink. They went to the Swiss Cottage bar in Santry. Over some toasted cheese sandwiches and pints of Carlsberg they caught up and had a few laughs about old times. The packed lounge bar, the background pop music, the Saturday sport fixture on the T.V. screen, the noisy and cheery surroundings and the alcohol all had almost a rehabilitative effect on Dave, offering him a short but relaxing remission from the ongoing trauma. He returned home that Saturday evening a chilled-out man.

"Where's Michael?" Harriet told him he was down at The Yacht Public House for a few scoops of Guinness. Lorena had gone on a date with a guy from work.

There was just the two of them in the house. "Which gives me a chance to talk with you Dave." They heard a crash of something upstairs. They ignored it. They were beginning to get used to this. "Let's go into the Dining Room, he bothers no one there."

"Yes, why IS that?" said Dave.

"Heaven knows," Harriet said. They sat down together. "Tell me Dave, what is it that makes you not run away like Sheila is about to do?"

"That's a bit harsh. She's scared. Who can blame her? Why don't you run away?"

"Now you and I both know we are not about to do that. We are made of the same cloth, you and I .We don't run."

"But it's more than that, isn't it Harriet? There is something deeper here that pervades both of us. We want to get to the truth of this. It doesn't sit well with us."

"This is true. No spirit or ghost or whatever it may be will see ME off! I won't be intimidated!"

"That's exactly the essence of you, Harriet. You are insulted by the audacity of this bastard. It goes to the core of you. You're internally strong, you refuse to be defeated."

"And you Mr. Molloy, you are infuriated. It is your anger. You won't let this absurdity win. Isn't that correct?" He smiled. "Yes! But Lorena doesn't have that. No anger."

"That's because Lorena is awed by the whole spectacle. She's enchanted. She has a great interest in metaphysics and the paranormal, for real, and clearly had before she came here. She is not in the least bit nervous. She sees herself as an explorer of these things. She embraces it all. She sees this as a golden opportunity. She loves it, the happenings I mean, the entire concept."

"Do you know what she does in her bedroom?"

"Yes I do David."

"Do you have a problem with that, Harriet?"

"No, because this enigma was already going on before she came here. Lorena and I have become good friends. Who knows, she might even help get rid of it." There were thudding footsteps on the stairs. Fast enraged ones. Harriet and Dave deliberately disregarded them. They were indeed birds of a feather. Together they would prove relentless against the foe.

On Sunday the sole event that occurred emanated from the closet under the stairs. It happened again. This time to Lorena. She went to turn on the hot water and discovered it on. But the switch suddenly began to turn on and off in front of her eyes without any movement from her. She was not happy. She said out loud, raising her head, "And I thought I was getting through to you, we were making progress. That's not cool man, that's not cool at all. Grow up!"

She telephoned Dave at his work on Monday afternoon. She was excited. In the background he could hear Dublin Airport announcements. "Last Call for Flight EI xxx to Paris, now departing at Gate 104."

"Dave my darlin' we have great news! The psychics are coming over. They got back to me today. Not too long a wait. Not bad. They're bringing equipment with them."

"When will they be here?"

"They'll be here on a Friday night. That way they can spend the weekend if they have to and we'll all be here. Well, except for Sheila of course."

"Which Friday, Lorena?"

"Well not until the 4th. of July, but they're coming!!!"

He thought for a minute. "That's about 11 days from now."

Around 6pm that same day, at home at 189 St. Bonaventure Road, Lorena told Michael about the forthcoming arrival of the English psychics. They were in the kitchen at the time. Harriet and Dave were present. "Isn't it great, Michael? Some professional experts on the way. Isn't it exciting? Give me a hug." She opened out her arms, happily, elated and approached Michael. He awkwardly responded. As they momentarily wrapped arms around each other, a force flung Michael backwards through the open kitchen door and into the hallway. He landed approximately 5 yards from where he had been hugging Lorena. They were shocked. All of them terrified. Everyone witnessed it. Michael was stunned. They helped him up. "Oh my God," cried Lorena. "Oh my God."

"Into the Dining Room, everybody," snapped Harriet. "INTO THE DINING ROOM, NOW!"

They sat there the four of them. Speechless. There was solitude in the stately Dining Room. Safety. They all knew it. They did not know why, but they knew it. They hoped it stayed that way. "Are you alright, Michael?" said Lorena, softly. "Fuck sake, what was that? It was some power I can tell you. I can't describe it. Christ, powerful! Why did it do it to ME?"

"Because I was hugging you. He's jealous."

"Ah for fuck sake, would your stop with your nonsense!" said Dave.

"It's not nonsense. He's protective of me. Don't you get it, all of you, he's protective of me!!" A startled silence.

"Okay, I agree, he's out of control now, this shouldn't have happened. I have something to tell you all." They waited for Lorena to elaborate. Not really wanting to hear what she would say.

"A few weeks ago, I don't know exactly when, a weeknight anyway, I was in bed about to go asleep. I felt my hair being touched. At first I didn't know what was going on, but then I knew for absolute certainty that my hair was being caressed. It ended after a while. It began after that." Dave felt a chill go down his spine. "What began?" asked Harriet.

"The touching, the caressing. It spread to my face. I'll admit it was terrifying at times. But other times it wasn't. It was almost soothing. Nothing else occurred. He never bothered me anywhere else, if you know what I mean."

"This is fucking nuts," said Dave.

Michael stood up. Without uttering a word he opened the Dining Room door, stepped out into the hallway and bellowed "YOU FUCKING BASTARD, YOU FUCKING PRICK, YOU COWARDLY BASTARD, SHOW YOUR FACE, FUCKING FIGHT ME MAN TO MAN, SHOW YOURSELF YOU PRICK." The house remained silent.

Michael ran upstairs in a terribly emotional state. After approximately five minutes, he returned with some personal items in a sports bag and entered the Dining Room. "I'm going to my real home. To my Dad's house." He was shaking visibly. "I'll stay in touch. I'm sorry." He walked out of the house instantly. They didn't think they'd see him again.

Sheila had been out apartment hunting.

By the time she came home a plan had already been put into action!

The resilience of three young people aged in their 20's in the face of tremendous adversity and terror in a house in Clontarf, Dublin City in 1986 is simply extraordinary. It is a story that has never been told, until now. Their dogged determination had deepened and was underway to an extent that would have astonished even them at an earlier time. Each of them had their own individual and separate reason for defiance.

One was a successful woman with a strong central belief system and calculating shrewdness. She would not be intimidated. It was abhorrent to her values. Another was resolute in his fortitude to combat the threat, to be unwavering in his response to evil, to be unbowed to fear. In the third was an awakening; a turn of events that challenged her charity and intuitiveness; that made her solidly committed to victory on behalf of her friends.

From the events of tonight they had discovered in themselves their own tenacity.

United they would be a force. What was about to happen in the next few hours in conjunction with the terror which had just occurred, would infuriate them and propel them into a war!

"Good to see you Sheila, did you have any luck out there trying to find a place?"

"It can take a while, Harriet." Sheila was not in good form. Unhappy to be back in the house and having to wait for Harriet to accompany her to her bedroom, she was already itchy, at a loose end. Dave, Lorena and Harriet had determined not to sleep alone in their own respective bedrooms. Following tonight's unexpected proceedings, they jointly decided that was now an absolute! Sheila had no inkling of what happened to Michael and barring any unforeseen circumstances ("which is always highly likely," said Dave) it was imperative not to tell her! If Sheila inquired as to where Michael was, they planned to lie and pretend he had gone to bed in his attic. But how would they conceal their teaming up at night from her? For Sheila's own state of mind, Harriet would go to her bedroom with her as before, where Harriet had a camping bed next to Sheila's bed and then Lorena and Dave would bunk down in the Dining Room. They would set an alarm clock to get themselves up before Sheila's arrival downstairs in the morning. It would only be for a few days until Sheila permanently left. Then after Sheila moved out, Harriet would also sleep in the Dining Room. They would get sleeping bags.

At 11:35pm Sheila and Harriet went upstairs to bed. As before, they slept in Sheila's room. Lorena and Dave waited; then quietly followed. Lorena grabbed her sleeping bag while Dave, who didn't have one, hurriedly snapped up a pillow, cover and sheet. They retreated downstairs into the Dining Room.

The house was still and quiet as the dark night slowly moved from hour to hour. Not a sound. The night drew closer to dawn. Dave and Lorena were jolted awake by a repetitive heavy-pounding sound upstairs. Very solid thuds, a constant pounding and within seconds "DAVE, DAVE, OH JESUS GOD IN HEAVEN, JESUS, LORENA, LORENA, DAVE, HELP US. AAAGH PLEASE HELP US." They charged up the stairs in answer to Harriet's voice. She had been on the Landing, shouting to downstairs. In Sheila's room amidst the clamour and horrendous banging, they could hear screams of "Absolute terror, blood-curdling screams piercing the air," coming from Sheila. They entered her room to a sight that will stay with them until their deaths. Harriet was standing by Sheila's bed screaming and praying. Sheila's bed was rising into the air and hitting the floor in unbroken repetitive constant succession. Sheila was in the bed and could not get out. She was being thrown into the air each time the bed rose and falling back into it when it hit the floor. The violence of the incident in its intensity was unspeakable. Sheila's screams were of such a nature that "You could not call them screams." "It was indescribable, terrifying." The rising and falling of her bed never ceased. Dave and Lorena desperately tried to grab her. Dave was powerfully thrown to the floor. Lorena kept trying. Harriet helped. Dave got up and tried again. He was furious. They eventually managed to drag her out and all four of them ran. As they did, the bed came to a stop.

Inside the Dining Room there were tears, shudders and silence. A full hour passed. Sheila spoke. "Get my bag and purse and keys." They looked at her but no one answered. They were still recovering. ‘Get my bag, purse and keys please.”

“Where are they?” said Dave, without thinking.

“In my room.”

No one questioned her. All three got up off the floor to their feet. “Let’s go!” said Dave.

Harriet, Dave and Lorena rushed up the stairs, charged into the room together and panic-stricken they rapidly found Sheila’s items, and in constant perpetual motion made it back to Sheila.

“Thank you. Goodbye.”

“What about your clothes?” said Lorena. No reply was forthcoming. Sheila placed her door keys upon the table. Without speaking she hurried down the hallway. They never saw her again.

As they got dressed and washed while clothed, the three of them stayed together in close proximity, Dave turning his back where appropriate. They left the house together at 8:20am. They walked to the seafront. The fresh morning air with the seagulls squawking above them brought a great sense of relief. They didn’t speak. They came upon a phone box. Harriet stepped in and called her Advertising firm. She said she wouldn’t be in today. Lorena phoned the airport and did likewise. Dave called and left a message for Carolyn and Frank.

Time passed. They continued walking along by Dublin Bay. Lorena started to quietly sing to herself. *"When I find myself in times of trouble, Mother Mary comes to me, speaking words of wisdom, let it be. And in my hour of darkness she is standing right in front of me, speaking words of wisdom, let it be. Let it be, oh let it be* Harriet and Dave joined in *yeah let it be, whisper words of wisdom, let it be. And when the night is cloudy, there is still a light that shines on me......................."*

They reached the long wooden bridge that led out onto the beach at Dollymount Strand. Without discussion, they found themselves wandering out to the sea. Sitting in the dunes, their hair windswept, the aroma of the Irish Sea refreshing them, Harriet turned and said "Houston, we have a problem." A moment's silence, a burst of laughter, erupted from three brave young people. United in their experience they began to talk. "I don't really want to go back there."

"Who does, Lorena?" said Dave. "I think we should stay away for a couple of days," Harriet opined. "We need a break, clear our heads and all of that."

"You're still determined then?"

"The séance is still to come and Harriet is to talk with the owner on Friday," said Lorena. "That's true and I'm damn well going to! My problem is though, that I really should be in work tomorrow and my family's home is in Limerick. How can I do that, I wonder?!"

"My family's in Cabra. You can stay there with me for a few days. And Dave, you can go to your family in Coolock."

"What day is today, Tuesday? We have the Abbey Theatre on Thursday night," said Dave. "Fine, we can still meet at Gallagher's for dinner before the Play and go to the Abbey from there," Harriet stated. "With two seats to spare," said Dave. 'I'll try and get the money back for Michael and Sheila's seats," said Harriet. "So, when are we going back to the house?"

"I don't know. Well I've to meet the owner on Friday, so will we give it a shot for Friday evening? We can all go in together and I'll fill you in on what transpires with my meeting at the bank" Nodding, they concurred.

They departed the beach and found themselves walking further down the Clontarf Road. There was a church nearby. St. Gabriel's. Dave suggested that they go in and say a prayer. "We're up against evil, why not give it a try,"' said Harriet. "How about you, Lorena?"

"Yes, that would be cool. I often pop in to churches." They knelt down in the pew. There, side by side they prayed. Their prayers merged as one, for strength to be bestowed upon them in their coming trials at 189 St. Bonaventure Road. Dave sat back in the pew. He had an idea. He whispered to the other two. "Let's get a priest. A priest to bless the house. Every room in it." Lorena whispered back, "You mean, like an exorcism?"

"No, I don't think they would do that. They have to get permission from the Vatican for that type of thing. Would take too long. No, I mean just to bless the whole house. It might work."

"Nothing ventured, nothing gained," whispered Harriet. They searched for a priest within the church but couldn't find one. They located the Presbytery door but there was no answer. They left the area. "I'm not giving up. I'll get a priest in our local church."

They were starving. They took a bus into the city centre and had a big feast in Flanagan's Restaurant on O'Connell St. "We need sleeping bags, one for Dave and one for me."

"The best place to get a sleeping bag is in a Scout Shop!" declared Lorena. There were two in the city. They found the nearest one. They procured one each for Harriet and Dave. With that, they parted. "See you Thursday night at Gallagher's," they said, as they waved Dave goodbye.

CHAPTER TWELVE

The next day Dave arrived at the office. He reiterated his excuse from the day before claiming he had been 'under the weather.' Carolyn offered to run to the shop and get him some warm soup. Feeling immeasurably guilty, he declined her kindness. He waited until Frank and Carolyn were on lunch to make the call to his local church. The priest's Housekeeper kept him on hold for a short while. "Hello, good afternoon, may I help you?"

"Yes Father, hello. I was wondering if you would come to our house to bless it."

"Do you live in our Parish?"

"Yes Father I do."

"Is there a particular reason you wish the house blessed?"

"No particular reason other than my family did the same when we moved into a new house when I was younger. Basically I'm the most recent tenant and I suggested it to my flatmates when I arrived. They have no objections and thought it would be nice."

"Ok, certainly, do you work Monday to Friday?"

"Yes I do, Father."

"Would Saturday morning be alright then, say about half-eleven?"

"That would be great.' Dave provided him with his name and the address. "Thank you Father, I appreciate it." He was never going to tell the priest the true reason for his request. Perhaps he would not come.

That night, for the second night in a row, Harriet, Dave and Lorena slept like the proverbial baby. On Thursday Frank and Dave had a meeting elsewhere in the city. On their way back to Baggot St. Frank insisted they drop in to O'Donoghue's Pub on Merrion Row for an afternoon pint. 'Looks like the perfect start to the rest of the day.'

They met at Gallagher's. Dave was the first one there. As he entered the doorway, he heard a familiar voice down the street. "Hey Dave, don't forget about me." It was Michael, hurrying down the footpath towards him. They got a booth and awaited the girls. "Delighted to see you Michael, I'm glad you came."

"I wouldn't miss it." Lorena and Harriet arrived. "Ah Michael, I'm so glad you're here," Lorena remarked, thrilled to see him there. They settled in. "Now, what are we going to order; Dave why don't you order your American food, something sophisticated, oh, I know, burger and fries," remarked Harriet, back to her sarcastic self. "I didn't come to Gallagher's to eat in New York; but pardon me maybe I'll just steal some of your ooh la la Moroccan chicken flowered with apricots, almonds and chickpeas, Harriet. Or perhaps I'll just wait till dessert and launch a gentlemanly assault on your Petits Pots a l'Absinthe!" She wasn't impressed. But for the second time in Harriet and Dave's personal interactions, she held a quiet smile of approval in her eyes. "Oh, would you two stop it!" said Lorena. "Michael, what are you going to have?"

"Well, after listening to all that, I'm going to have a bar-b-cue cheese burger and fuck the begrudgers." They all chuckled, Harriet included.

"So Michael, how are you feeling after what happened the other night?"

"Obviously, not great. I learned one thing Lorena, never hug you. In fact, I'd be afraid to even look at you in that house again!"

"I'm so sorry Michael."

"It's not your fault. You had no way of knowing."

They told him they had left the house until Friday night. They didn't inform him however, of the catastrophic event that had occurred with Sheila. "Why did you leave, because of what that bastard did to me?"

"Yes, we got to thinking about it and decided to step away for a while," replied Dave. They did notify him that Sheila was permanently gone. "I don't blame her, not one bit!"

"I was wondering Michael, are you just here for tonight or would you consider coming back?"

"I don't know. It's been only three days, Lorena."

"I'll fill you in," said Harriet. "The status of everything as of this moment is I am meeting with the owner tomorrow. I'm going to grill her on this. We are returning to Bonaventure Road tomorrow evening.

The séance is scheduled for tomorrow week..."*Dave.. interrupting..*"that's not all, the priest is coming on Saturday morning."

"You got a priest?" said Michael, encouraged. "Yes, as you can see, we're fighting back on all fronts."

Lorena was excited, "What time on Saturday?"

"11:30." Dave wanted Michael back.

"So you see Michael, we have Harriet's meeting with the owner, the séance, the Catholic Church. "A three-pronged approach for information-gathering and a good strong retaliation against this evil prick. It might, possibly could, get rid of him. The blessing of the house or the séance or both."

"If you don't hug me, if no one hugs me or anything like that, he'll have no reason to throw you or anyone to the ground, Michael," added Lorena. Dave looked at Harriet. There was a mutual understanding between them. There was no reason for what happened to Sheila! Or was there? In the world of evil, in another dimension crisscrossing into ours carrying a demonic aspect with it, at least in this case, the case of Sheila, was there a reason? A reason, thus far, only known to the perpetrator.

"There might be something to what you say, Dave. I don't know. I'll think on it. I felt bad leaving you all. And I must admit, I'm missing you bastards already, although for the life of me, I have no idea why!" Laughter. "If you do come back, we're definitely all sleeping together in the Dining Room in sleeping bags, you can forget your attic," said Dave. "Yes, what is it about the Dining Room, it's so peaceful in there. There's a sense of calm, tranquility even. In a normal house you don't even get that!"

"Don't know the why's and if's Lorena, but it's true. Even in the midst of pounding and banging and all that hatred, the room is unaffected."

"It's our sanctuary," said Harriet.

"With Sheila gone and hopefully not you Michael, our rent individually will increase to meet the monthly amount," continued Harriet. "Shouldn't we get another renter?" inquired Lorena. 'With where this equation is at now, I don't think it would be responsible of us to do that. What do you think, Dave?"

"No, probably not a good idea. Not for now, anyway."

"I'll be honest, my compadres, I don't think I can cover the extra," said Lorena. "Pay what you're paying now, and if you agree Dave, you and I can make up the difference between us," suggested Harriet. "Sure will," said Dave. "If I come back, I will too. My rent is paid up until the end of June and I'll let you know by tomorrow if I'm paying for July," said Michael. Harriet still had the two extra tickets for the Theatre and gave one to Michael.

"The performance commences in 15 minutes," came the announcement. "Please take your seats. Flash photography and eating or consuming of beverages is not permitted. This is the 15 minute Call. Please take your seats. Thank you." The crowd began to filter from the Abbey Theatre's Bar into the plush auditorium. Harriet had forgotten to seek a refund for Sheila's ticket and before she could inquire, Lorena grabbed it from her. She went to the small queue for people looking for on-the-night last minute cancellations and seeing a gentleman on his own approached him. "It's on me" she said with a warm smile as she handed him the ticket.

The dialogue on stage continued. *"You'd sell your soul to the devil for a cup of buttermilk."* Lorena was engrossed. Michael sat there joyously enjoying John B. Keane's script. His inimitable conjuring of sentences. *"He has the health of a spring salmon."* But Dave's thoughts were elsewhere, meandering off into what the future held for them at 189 St. Bonaventure Road. He leaned over to Harriet sitting next to him. He whispered in her ear. "The incident with Sheila occurred at 4:50am. Exactly the same time as one of the other incidents. One that happened five days before. They're not all at the same time but those two were.4:50am exactly!" She turned and whispered back, "Sometimes I wonder about you Dave, but I'm glad you're doing those calculations. There might be something to it. Maybe."

FRIDAY, JUNE 27TH.

Harriet rang Dave. "I'm meeting Lorena in the City Centre. My guess is we'll be at the house about six. Don't go in until we meet outside. We'll do the same. The three of us will go in together. We're bringing extra food, tins of beans, pears, crisps, chocolate, that type of thing. We have wine too. Just in case no one wants to go to the kitchen at any time.

"How did it go with the Landlady?" Dave asked.

"I'll tell you tonight."

They met Dave outside the house. From the gate, they watched up the long narrow pathway, the black-painted front door looking ominous and imposing at the pathway's end. "Alright, I suggest this," said Harriet. "When we first go in, we go to our rooms and take anything we need; passports, mementos, bank books, clothes, shoes, general valuables. Keep them with us in the Dining Room. Because if any mayhem starts, we can run out the door with everything we need. If that happens, I am never coming back. I'm getting a train down to Limerick tonight!"

"Got it!" declared Lorena.

They went inside. They were an uncomfortable but very determined trio. They put the belongings they had with them into the large dignified Dining Room and went upstairs. They succeeded, in a very nervous state, checking on each other constantly, in achieving Harriet's objective. They returned to the stately room with everything. They went to the kitchen together, cooked a small meal for themselves and brought it with them into the Dining Room. They closed the door behind them. Alongside all their goods, they had a radio and flashlights. They tuned the radio to a pop music channel and settled down.

The front door opened. "DAVE, LORENA, HARRIET, IF YOU'RE HERE LET ME KNOW. I'M NOT COMING IN UNLESS YOU ANSWER." Dave hurried to the hallway. "No need to shout, we're here. We're all here."

They were glad to have Michael back. He had grit and felt a certain loyalty to them. There were four of them now. In that, they felt better.

"As you all know, I met with the owner at the bank today. I deposited the money as always, so there'd be a record."

"What did she say?" insisted Lorena, impatiently.

"I started out by asking her how old this house is. She said she didn't know the exact year it was built, but she believes it was the late 1880's or 1890's. She wanted to know why I was asking. I wouldn't tell her at first. I was afraid she'd bottle up. I just kept on talking and asked if she'd ever lived here? She said no. She said she bought it from someone else and decided to rent it out as a house share. I asked her had there been many tenants before us? She said there had been four people sharing the house before I came. I asked her what happened to them? She got annoyed with me and said "How would I know?!!" I asked her were those four people here at the same time and she said "Yes they were and what's all this about, Harriet?" I kept in her face and asked her why did they leave and how long was it between their departure and my arrival? Although she's a very refined lady and up to now has been nothing but respectful and nice to me, she got really pissed off with me. I asked her twice why did they leave? She just looked at me with a blank stare and said nothing. So I just said it like it is. I told her some of what's been going on here and asked her straight to her face did she know that her house is haunted?!!!"

"What did she say?!" said Michael.

"She was quiet for a minute and then said if we want to leave we should just do so. Then she walked away, left me standing there."

'She fucking knows it's haunted! She knew before you even got here, Harriet."

"Looks like it, Dave," said Harriet with a wry smile.

"Oh, what to do, what to do," Lorena sighed.

"Well, this is how I see it," stated Harriet. "We've paid up for July. By the way Michael, if you're staying you owe me for July. So it's our choice to walk out or stay for another month. Or, as David and Lorena hope, between the priest and the séance, we'll make him go away, or as Lorena says, make him go bye bye into the next dimension. We all adore this house, it's beautiful but we have to live in it. He has to be disposed of. I say we stay and give the church and the séance a go."

"So do I" said Dave.

"Me too," said Lorena.

"I'm with you," said Michael. "I hate the bastard."

Nothing dreadful plagued that night. The dark hours passed peacefully. They slept in their sleeping bags with some trepidation, yet were undisturbed. The dawn advanced, the sun rose in the sky, but no birds would sing in the garden at 189 St. Bonaventure Road.

SATURDAY, JUNE 28TH.

"Let's all have breakfast together in the kitchen. Far nicer than bringing it in here." Sunny mornings have a way of delivering confidence to precarious conditions. They establish a psychology of new refreshment, new promising commencements. An inauguration of illumination if only for a few hours or until grey clouds interfere with the joy of sunlight. "Yes, let's do that Harriet," exclaimed Lorena. Over boiled eggs and toast with marmalade, they discussed the impending arrival of the priest. "What are we telling him when he comes?" asked Michael. "I'll tell you what we are going to do! We're going to do nothing! Tell him nothing! Just keep to what I told him on the phone. We want the house blessed for the same reason as some old lady down the country wants it. Tradition!"

"If we level with him before he starts, he might run out the fucking door," said Lorena. "Just let him do his job, let him go around in any order he likes," said Dave. "He's probably used to this type of request."

"Not in a house like this he's not!" declared Michael. Harriet and Lorena went upstairs together to the bathroom to wash. Then Dave and Michael. Sheila's bedroom door was wide open. Dave rushed over and shut it.

10:50am: A noise came from the living room. Harriet and Dave investigated. The television was on the floor, the screen face down.

11:02am: A crashing sound upstairs sounded to them as if it came from Sheila's bedroom but they couldn't be sure; Harriet's room was also a possibility at the time.

11:04am: They could hear a door repeatedly opening and slamming shut upstairs. It sounded to them as either Dave's bedroom door or the bathroom door adjoining it. Dave continued to log the times.

11:13am: They needed to pick the T.V. off the floor before the arrival of the priest. As they entered the hall to return to the Dining Room both Lorena and Dave saw the telephone fall from the small table. "You could literally see it being pushed." Lorena replaced it!

11:24am: A knock on the front door. "Hello, I'm Father ---------."

"Hello Father, thanks for coming." When Dave answered the door and greeted him, the other three were standing behind him. The priest appeared to look perplexed, perhaps usually one doesn't get four people standing eagerly awaiting a priest's arrival in a hallway. He didn't appear to dwell on it. "Well, I'll let you do your thing, sorry Father, I mean...Bless the house." The priest smiled. He was a young curate, in everyday clerical dress, his clothes impeccably neat and pressed. "I'm just going into every room, I'll bless it. If you could lead the way," he said to Dave.

Before they began the priest said, "Peace to this Household."

Dave walked into the Living Room. The priest walked past him into the middle of the room and sprinkling Holy Water he stated, "In nomine Patris et Filii et Spiritus Sancti." (In the name of the Father, Son and Holy Spirit). He then proceeded back into the hallway. Dave swallowed hard, desperately grateful nothing had occurred to the priest in there. Yet Dave, like the rest, almost hoped something would occur. A validation of sorts to another human being, especially a priest of the Holy Church, that they were in turmoil. As he walked, each of them was silently and desperately pleading in their heart for help. The priest turned right to enter the hallway and was automatically facing the closed kitchen door. He jolted back. Saying nothing, he continued on. "In nomine Patris et Filii et Spiritus Sancti." He exited the Dining Room and Dave, opening the door for him, walked ahead of him into the kitchen. There was a silence. Dave looked back. The priest was standing on the cusp of the kitchen, not entering. "Everything alright?" said Dave. The young curate did not answer but went ahead and entered the kitchen. "In nomine Patris et Filii (*his voice rose and strengthened*) et Spiritus Sancti." The kitchen's temperature dropped rapidly, significantly in seconds. A wooden chair against the table flew across the room crashing against the stove. Each witnessed it. The priest's face turned ashen. But he stood his ground. Trembling, he said again; loudly from the beginning this time. "IN NOMINE PATRIS ET FILII ET SPIRITUS SANCTI."

They ran into the hall. "You have a presence in this house. Why didn't you tell me!!!!!?" The priest was fuming. Shaking, he didn't wait for Dave. He ran upstairs and they saw him entering Dave's room. No one followed him! Blessing the room, he did likewise in the bathroom. As he went up the few steps to the Landing, and now being out of sight of everyone at the base of the staircase, they could hear the familiar but hideous banging of Sheila's bed upon the floorboards. They heard the young priest's piercing scream. They assumed he had opened the door. The priest came running back down to them. In what took about 20 seconds in its entirety, the following occurred: The priest, horror-stricken, said to them "Leave here! Do not stay here. For God's sake, leave!" He faced the length of the hallway. He declared to the house "PATER FILIUS ET SPIRITUS SANCTUS SUNT IN NOMINE DOMINI." He then immediately left.

They went into their sanctuary room. "Wow!" said Lorena. All was quiet. Harriet proposed they go for a walk. They went to St. Anne's Park nearby. Amidst the cyclists, baby strollers, joggers and Frisbee enthusiasts, they sat on the grass. "I should have told him," said Dave. "I really should."

"What's done is done," said Michael. "He's got to be pure evil, he freaked out when the priest was there."

"Well I think we know what he is by now, Harriet, this fella is really bad news."

"Does anyone think the blessing will have a positive effect in the long run? It should but I'm not so sure."

"Hard to tell Harriet, there's a chance," said Dave.

"There's no chance!" said Lorena. 'No chance at all."

Lying there on the grass for approximately two hours, they unwound from the morning's occurrences. Returning to the seafront they grabbed something to eat in a local Chip Shop. They sat and ate at a window countertop. Bonnie Tyler's *'Total Eclipse of the Heart'* was playing in the background when Harriet said, "How in the name of God is the séance going to help us? If that was the result today, I don't see how. The séance is secular. Today was religious. What possible gain can we expect from a séance? He was frantic when Father what's his name was there, in fact he knew he was coming, see what happened just before he came?! How the hell did he know that?!! But he did! I just cannot understand how a séance works in our favour. He'll probably laugh at it!"

"I think he listens to us. I just know he does. That's why he knew the priest was coming," said Lorena. "That scared him. Bothered the shit out of him. There IS power in the Church. That's why he lost it. But I'm afraid it didn't budge him. It wasn't enough. You'd need a full exorcism. That's why there's no chance right now, not until we do that. But the séance can tell us more."

"How?" asked Dave.

"We'll have professionals with us. They'll conduct it. They'll know what they are doing. This is what they do for a living. They'll make contact."

"They won't have to! He'll make contact with them," sniggered Michael, "and it won't be pretty."

"Yes, maybe he will, but they'll be prepared for it. They'll draw him in and try and get the info. Why he's here, why won't he move on, what does he want, if anything? They might have the tools, the skills to move him on. They're used to dealing with spirits. They'll advise us. Tell us how to operate. What to do to get rid of him, if they don't do it themselves on the night!"

"Oh Lorena, what are we to do with you?" said Harriet, "it should be interesting I guess. But I can tell you, if they want to do it in Sheila's bedroom I'm not going in. You can take that to the bank. I swear, you won't find me in there."

"Me neither," said Dave.

They made their way back. They spent the rest of the day hanging out in the back garden and the Dining Room, scurrying the kitchen between both without incident.

On Sunday, Dave spent the day at his folks' residence. He interacted with his family, enjoying a Sunday dinner of Roast Chicken, Roast Potatoes, peas and carrots. He thoroughly relished a post-dinner afternoon nap in the spare bed upstairs; a respite from his sleeping bag. He didn't really want to go back to Clontarf that night but wouldn't let the other three down. Before he departed, he spent a little time with his father, whom he dearly loved. They had grown closer since Dave had returned from America. They were discussing the affairs of the day when Dave said "Hey Dad, can I talk with you about something?" His father looked at him disquietingly. He hoped he wasn't about to be informed that Dave was heading back to America sooner than expected. "Dad, I never heard you mention anything about, well, you know, things about ghosts or spirits or that kind of topic."

"Why would I?"

"I don't know, I guess you'd have no reason."

His Dad laughed. "What are you on about, David?"

"Ah, nothing."

"Hold on a minute, what are you getting at?" His Dad thought the matter amusing. "I suppose I'll just be up front with you Dad, we have a ghost in Clontarf."

"You mean, where you live? In the house where you live?"

"Yes." He waited for his father to say there were no such things as ghosts. But he didn't. "What makes you think that?" Without going into detail Dave referred to a few of the lesser incidents they had suffered. All his father said was "Well, what do you want to do?" Dave was astounded. His Dad had no questions other than that. Did his father believe him? He wasn't sure. "You can come home here anytime you like. Your mother and myself would be happy to have you."

"Alright, I'll keep that in mind. Thanks." As he left he was happy to hear his father say "If you need anything, call. If you want me to come down in the car and get you anytime day or night, just call."

CHAPTER THIRTEEN

MONDAY, JUNE 30TH.

Dave left for work. Walking down the pathway to the gate a force hit him, right where the leg meets the front of the foot sending him tripping and then falling forwards. Getting a shock, he quickly proceeded to the gate and walked on, never turning back. He remembered Michael saying something similar had been done to him. Except it hadn't quite hit Dave, more readily been waiting for him. Like a stationary invisible presence.

That evening upon his return home (and straight into the Dining Room), Michael and Lorena told him to go to the Living Room.

"Why?"

"You'll see," said Michael. He hesitantly walked in. The two couches were standing vertical in the centre of the room. Books were scattered across the carpet. The book shelf was devoid and bare of its literary works. The television, stereo system, and coffee table were out of place. Indeed the two electrical items were lying away from each other on the floor. Knickknacks from the mantelpiece lay horizontally across the room. "Now go into the kitchen," said Michael, "and before you do, keep in mind that I was home first and the front door and back door were both locked." He nervously went in. Water was steadily running from both taps. Across the kitchen from there, a pool of water stood just inside the door. The glass on the back door was comprehensively smashed with one end of the kitchen table lying sideways through it. Pots, pans and kitchen dishes were strewn everywhere. Some dishes were in pieces. "This is how I found it and I touched nothing. I want you all to see, for fuck sake," said Michael. Harriet was soon home and they left it all, as is, for her to view. "This is increasing rapidly," said Lorena, "I can't wait for the séance." Her comments sent shudders up three spinal cords!

When Tuesday evening arrived, Lorena answered a telephone call in the hall. The others stayed in their sanctuary room. After about 20 minutes she returned to them. "The Psychic group phoned."

"They are still coming, aren't they?"

"Yes, of course they are Harriet. They'll be here on Friday as planned."

"What did they want?" said Dave.

"They wanted as much detail as possible before they get here."

"What kind of detail?"

"The fella I spoke with was a man named Steven. He wanted me to go over again everything I told them previously. He said to try to remember as much as possible about all the incidents including the ones I told him already. He also wanted information on anything that happened since we last spoke with them. He explained it was vital not to leave anything out. He was big on that."

"Are they actually staying the weekend?" asked Michael. "Yes they said they would anyway."

"In this house, or a B. & B. or hotel or something?"

"Here in the house. Although he did say, if the séance was quiet and there was no activity by Saturday afternoon they might leave early."

"I suspect he's just being cautious. Making sure they're not wasting their time, ensuring we're on the up and up and all that," said Harriet.

"That's why he asked me to repeat everything I said before. He was checking me out. He asked me all your names again. Your full names. What do we all work at etcetera? Just to make sure everything matched from our earlier conversations."

"How many are coming," inquired Dave. "Two, three, four?"

"I don't know, I forgot to ask."

"Are they bringing equipment like you said they were?"

"Yes, but I've no idea exactly what."

"So, it's a séance AND equipment. They're thorough!"

"I hope they prove to be," added Harriet.

"He said they'd be here late afternoon. We'll have to get off work early, except for you Michael, you should be finished your shift by then."

"God help me, yes," said Michael.

As it does in June in Ireland the brightness remained late into the day, so to escape the Dining Room for a while, they all sat in the back garden talking and whiling away the time. At 4:50am the next morning doors slammed throughout the residence. It sounded to them there were almost simultaneous slams at differing doors in different parts of the house. The Dining Room door behind which all were ensconced never moved nor made a sound.

As Harriet left for work she received the mail from the postman. One letter was addressed to Dave. She left it on the hall table. He saw it and being in a rush, took it to Baggot. St. with him. "You're not yourself Dave, is he Carolyn?"

"What do you mean, Frank?"

"You're not as sharp at your work as you have been."

"Christ, Frank, that's a bit harsh."

"Let's face it brother, you're a bit cranky lately, not up to standard, not yourself at all, not the Dave I know!" Carolyn remained stoic in keeping with her modus operandi but there was a glint of agreement in her eye. "Listen you two, I'm fine. A few things on my mind that's all. Nobody's perfect. But I'll get back on target Frank, I promise you."

"Just stay focused Dave, that's all I ask."

Dave delved into his duties somewhat more that day, that is until he opened the letter. It was from the priest.

There was a note inside the envelope. 'David, please phone me right away. I want to speak with you. I don't have your number. Call between 3 and 5pm. Regards,....'

"Hello Father, this is David Molloy."

"Thanks for calling me. David, it is a must that you and the others leave that house immediately. The fact that you phoned me tells me you are still there. You got my letter. I'm sorry but I cannot go back there again. You have an evil and vile entity within that house and it is foolhardy in the extreme to stay in that dwelling. I have discussed this with my fellow priests. They, of course, are of the same mind. You must leave. Surely, you all have alternative accommodation. Families of your own and the like."

"Father, I am sorry for what you went through last Saturday. I'm particularly sorry for not forewarning you. I thought you could help us. I'm not blaming you or the Church; I think an exorcism is the key here but I know you don't allow that too often."

"Only certain key people connected directly to the Vatican can okay that David, and to tell you the truth the Irish Church doesn't have much of that, let me put it that way. I'm not saying I'm against that, but you're better off just leaving!"

"Okay Father, I understand. We just want to put up a fight, if that makes any sense to you."

"You're not in a position to do that, David. I can't believe you said that! But there's something I want to tell you. I consulted with others. There is an older priest, I won't say who, that remembers that house. He was called there many years ago. He is retired now and has left this parish. He experienced what I did. All I will tell you is that a suicide occurred there, a suicide by hanging. In the 1940's. Just leave the house David, you and your friends."

Dave bolted into an alertness. "So you're saying that the priest wasn't called to the house when that hanging happened, but later?"

"Look David, clearly most suicides do not cause hauntings regardless of how the person committed the act; but in this particular case, well, who knows? It is believed there are hauntings from natural deaths as well, and whether natural death or suicide, such events remain rare. I am asking you to leave for your own well-being and the well-being of the other three persons I met there."

"I know you're right Father, the reality is I don't think we can stay much longer, perhaps we ARE foolhardy, but thank you for everything and this information." The priest closed the call by re-stating his plea that the house be vacated. When Dave hung-up, he was met by Carolyn and Frank staring at him in disbelief. 'Oh God, thought Dave, 'Oh God.'

"You are seriously joking me Dave! Is that what's been going on?"

"Listen Frank, *interruption by Frank* "You don't really believe all that crap, do you Dave!? Ah hold the horses, stop the wagons, you gotta be shittin' me! Should I start singin' *'Casper the Friendly Ghost'* around here?!"

"Go fuck yourself," said Dave, as he walked out of the office!

It was 4:45pm approximately when Dave rang the doorbell at the Presbytery. "Can I speak to Father......' please?"

"I'm afraid he's having his tea at the moment," the Housekeeper replied. "Tell him it's Dave Molloy. I need to see him."

"He can't see people without an appointment."

"I'm telling you now to let me see him!" he demanded. "He'll know what it's about and he'll want to see me!"

She closed the door on Dave, having reluctantly told him to wait. The priest came to the door. "I'm sorry about that, she's a little protective of me and my schedule," he said, smiling. "Come on in David." He led him to a Sitting Room. "I've come for more information to be frank, Father. Anything you can tell me about the hanging."

"Look David, I've told you all you need to know. Just get out of that evil house!"

"All I need to know?? Father, I'm living this problem, day in and day out. I've already lost a day at work and today I walked out in the middle of the afternoon and I'm probably in serious trouble with my boss now. All because of this and how it's affecting me. All I need to know? Father, with all respect to you I'm entitled to know more. Anything you've learned about this, I should know."

"Okay David, what I have gleaned is because, after my own experience there, I started to ask questions. I was eventually put on to a retired Father who worked here for a while 30 years or so ago. He did not attend on the day the poor fellow was found but was called to the house ultimately for the same reason I was. Whatever happened on his visit, he asked questions too and discovered from a colleague, a fellow priest, about the hanging in the house 10 years or so prior to that. Did you get all that, David?"

"Thanks Father. Ok, so this definitely happened 40 years ago, the actual hanging I mean."

"Approximately 40 years ago. It was during the Emergency (WW2 period)."

"And the priest arrived about 30 years ago to bless the house?"

"Yes, obviously the occupants asked for him."

"So this problem was already happening in the 1950's?"

"Clearly, yes."

"So here's my million dollar question, Father. Where in the house did the hanging occur?"

"He was told the kitchen. In the kitchen."

Dave went silent. The priest allowed the silence to pass as Dave took it all in.

"Are you sure it wasn't a murder, Father?"

"I was told that it was not."

"And you're sure it was a man, although I've never imagined otherwise?"

"Yes, I was informed that the person found dead in the kitchen was male. A big male. A large big fellow. I will say however, that doesn't mean that the person who died is the entity that is in the house now. It probably is though."

Dave again drew silent. "David, I know no more and that's a fact. Isn't that enough for you? Haven't you and that other lad and the two girls there suffered enough? For Christ's sake man, protect yourselves! Leave!"

Dave walked home from there. He believed they were in a better position with this further knowledge. But he was bereft as to how that position could be of ultimate benefit. 'My God. A hanging! A fellow hung himself in the house. Why? Money? Gambling? Depression? All of that? Something else? Over a woman? Who knows!? And in the kitchen! A big man would need a strong rope I would think. Oh Lord, what am I thinking?! I'm consumed with this. I'm getting out after this séance on Friday.'

He sat the others down and related what he learned from the priest and how it all transpired today. Lorena offered her condolences on what evolved at Dave's job. "They'd never understand, don't even try to explain to them, Dave," stated Michael. "This all explains why the kitchen is so active," said Lorena, "but how does that jive with Sheila's bedroom?"

"He surely didn't like poor Sheila," said Harriet.

"And then there's the living room, the stairs, the Landing, the hallway. It's everywhere," added Lorena.

"The bathroom, the attic, inside my bedroom and inside your room Harriet, all so far seem unaffected," said Dave. But nowhere was there peace like the Dining Room. The sanctuary. The shelter from the inferno.

Following their Dining Room dinner, Lorena and Harriet went to the back garden to get fresh air and for something to do out there, started weeding. Michael produced twelve bottles of Carlsberg and putting them on the table said, "You and me Dave are going to mellow out before that prick throws his temper-tantrums again!" Out in the garden the girls were chatting away, pulling weeds and feeling somewhat liberated from their sanctuary room. Birds always tweet as they nest down at twilight but as Harriet and Lorena worked in the garden, the only avians they could hear were in the distant vicinity of other houses. No bird utterances were to be heard in their immediate surroundings. Lorena felt a blow of air in her right ear. Then her hair was yanked from behind, violently drawing her head backwards. Screaming, she ran across the grass to Harriet and together they rushed indoors. Once inside, she was in a panic, shaking. They calmed her and Harriet filled her full of red wine. At 10:20pm Dave and Michael went together to the kitchen. While there they looked up at the ceiling wondering about the hanging. "Maybe he didn't use anything that was up there," said Michael. "Some makeshift situation at the time, long gone now." The four of them went upstairs to the bathroom as they did every night just before sleeping. They would take turns going in with three waiting outside. This is how they lived now. Dave took a peek into his bedroom next door. How he missed his bed and privacy and a proper night's rest. The large parakeet green carpet looked lonesome, staring back up at him. No one walked upon it now. Not Dave anyway. The night passed without further incident.

CHAPTER FOURTEEN

THURSDAY, JULY 3RD.

On the way to work, Dave stopped in at a coffee shop and purchased pastries for the three of them. 'Try to soften the blow for what is coming next.' As always, Carolyn was there first. "Dave, about yesterday, do you really have a presence or something in your house? I don't mean to pry and I didn't want to say anything in front of Frank."

"Yes Carolyn, I DO have a presence in the house!"

"We were really taken aback by your phone call, we couldn't help but hear. You have to admit it's not every working day that type of conversation develops in an office environment. You can't really blame

Frank but I was thinking about it at home last night and I want you to know I believe you."

"Oh you do, do you? Well I hope you do because it's true. I'm sorry Carolyn, I've been under a bit of pressure with this to the point where I let my guard down in here yesterday. Here, have a pastry, those coconut ones are good," he said, trying to normalize the situation.

"Dave, you'd be surprised but I have a keen curiosity in the supernatural. I do a bit of reading on those kinds of topics and always have done."

"Believe me Carolyn, don't dig too deep. It may sound interesting to you and it is, but it can be horrifying depending on what type of thing you're dealing with. Terrifying as a matter of fact." Carolyn had a sympathetic, almost motherly look upon her face. "Anyway, I can't stay there much longer, I'm getting out but I appreciate your support. I'm really sorry about my language yesterday and walking out." She nodded and could see he didn't wish to pursue this particular discussion any further. She asked no additional question.

Frank arrived and as he walked by Dave sitting at his desk he broke into loud song, '*Casper the friendly ghost, the friendliest ghost you know. Though grown-ups might look at him with fright, the children all love him so.'* "Ah, for God's sake Frank, knock it off!"

"Why should I knock it off? My employee, vital to the company, vital to our general operations, my business confidante and friend took over our office yesterday with announcements of ghostly sightings and all things paranormal. Oh, no, ladies and gentlemen our new slogan here at the Representative Office is 'We do polls and analysis on all ghostly appearances. Statistical reports within a day for your ghoulish pleasure. Jesus, we'll clean up. They'll love us back in New York!" Then he began again *'Casper the friendly ghost, he couldn't be bad or mean. He'll romp and play, sing and dance all day, the friendliest ghost you've seen.'* He quickly turned to Carolyn. "Carolyn, would you do me a favour? Would you please go for a walk. Take an hour to yourself, have a coffee or shop or whatever you want to do." Carolyn hurriedly took off.

"YOU GOD DAMN LISTEN TO ME DAVE. IF YOU EVER WALK OUT OF HERE AGAIN, YOU'RE DONE. IT'S OVER. YOU'D NEVER GET AWAY WITH THAT BACK IN NEW YORK. "Got it boss, got it. No argument. I apologize for yesterday." Frank quietened his approach. "You don't really believe that stuff Dave, do you?"

"I won't ever lose my cool in here again boss, I give you my word and apologies, but whether you accept it or not, yes, we have a supernatural, call it what you want, presence, in our rented house."

"I love ya like a brother Dave and you've been very helpful to me in everything, both here in the office and in all we do. You're a professional at this game and we do great together. I won't be reporting this to Head Office. Don't blow it though. If you don't I see no further difficulty. I like ya lots. Keep your feet on the ground."

"Will do, Frank." No more was said.

Late in the afternoon Eddie rang Dave. He had dropped off a fare in the city centre and figured he'd wrap it up for the day. He wanted to know if Dave would go for a pint with him after work. They went to the Goalpost Bar on Cathedral St. Eddie dropped him home about 9pm. He rushed straight up the stairs to the bathroom to offload, bursting to use the toilet. Subsequently, as the four of them got into their sleeping bags, Lorena told him of footsteps on the stairs about 7:45pm. It gave him quivers thinking he had been on the stairs not much later.

FRIDAY, JULY 4TH.

The psychics would be arriving possibly around 4 or 5pm. Dave hadn't mentioned it to Lorena, Harriet or Michael but he now was not prepared to quit work early, as all had agreed they would do. His employment was far too important. He had put it in jeopardy only two days ago and to depart early now would be his death knell. He would return home at the normal time.

But when he entered the house at about 6:15pm, they had still not shown. "Where are they?"

"Well, where were you?" said an angry Harriet.

"Long story, sorry."

"They phoned from the airport. They wanted to have a bit of grub before they came on here. Probably enjoying themselves. We're sitting here like idiots", said Michael. “It doesn’t matter guys, at least they’re on their way,” Lorena said. Fifteen minutes later they were at the door.

“Hello there, is there a Lorena here?”

“Yes, I’m Lorena,’ she said, stepping forward. Steven shook her hand. “Nice to meet you in person Lorena, and you must be Harriet, Dave and Michael.” Standing with him in the hall were a man and woman. “This is Judith and Kenny, part of the team.”

“Do you have gear with you?” asked Michael.

“Yes we do, it’s outside in the rental car. We’ll leave it there for a few minutes while we take a look around, if that’s alright.” Lorena escorted them straight to the Dining Room. “Cup of tea for everyone?” she inquired. “I’ll go with you,” said Harriet, “after all, it IS the kitchen.”

“I’ll come along if I may,” Judith interjected. The girls were only too happy to have her. Judith, like the two men with her, appeared to be in her thirties. Kenny possessed a definitive London Cockney accent whereas the other two sounded like they were fresh off the cricket fields at Eton. Steven and Kenny were anxious to explore the house but considered it prudent to wait for the tea. "So did the other person here leave?" Steven glanced at a notebook. "Sheila I believe, yes, I think Lorena mentioned to me on the phone that she had left the house?"

"She did indeed," replied Dave, "for obvious reasons."

"This is a rather grand room. I presume we're in the Dining Room or what Lorena referred to as the Sanctuary Room."

"That's exactly why we're here. Sanctuary!"

The girls came in with seven teas on a tray. "Ooh, seven cups," said Michael, "the lucky and Angelic number. A good number to begin with. Let me tell you lads, you'll be needin' it!" he said to the visitors. Steven glimpsed at Judith. "Well, any first impressions?"

"Temperature in the kitchen not in accordance with rationale. Not at all."

"How low?"

"Bordering on freezing." Turning to the occupants Steven said, "I presume this was not the case prior to the happenings here."

"Of course it was," said Michael, "we all wanted to move into a house with a glacier for a kitchen. I dreamed of it as a child. I'm thinking of raising Polar Bears here."

"That's ENOUGH, Michael," demanded Harriet.

"Okay everyone, we're here to help you. If we can all work to some kind of script together it shall benefit us multilaterally. Michael, I understand your frustrations. I have seen the tensions that can rise between people in these scenarios. A presence in a house has the means of altering everyone and everything unequivocally. We are here to assist and solve things, if is at all attainable."

Addressing Lorena he stated, "Lorena, I'd like you to tell the team your own experiences with this. Include anything you have not admitted to your friends here before."

"Jesus man, they know everything. I've never tried to hide anything, other than keeping it from Dave for a while, to let him settle in and maybe to protect him in my own way, I guess. But if you've told Judith and Kenny everything I told you, then everyone here in this room is on the same page regarding me."

"Harriet?"

"I always say it as I see or experience it. There was one very unpleasant episode I personally endured alone in the kitchen. But I want to make very clear here, I shall not be discussing it with any person in this room whatsoever. Don't ask me about it. Otherwise I have reported everything to everyone. I'm sure Lorena informed you of anything concerning me alone and of course, most things have occurred in the presence of two or more of us."

"Dave?"

"Everyone knows everything I've experienced with them present and I always tell the others anything that happens to me alone, in or around this house. But, well, maybe there is something I haven't brought up. I don't think it has any effect on this though."

"What's that, Dave?" said Steven.

"Two things." He told them quickly about his U.F.O. encounter in San Francisco; then as he started to relate the Brooklyn story, the loud noise of footsteps pounding the stairs commenced. "Anyone else in the house?" said Steven alarmingly. The occupants looked at him calmly as if to say "There you go, see? We told you."

"No one else here but 'you know who'," said Lorena.

The three English investigators ran into the hallway and looked up the stairs. The pounding continued in their immediate domain. The pounding ceased. They returned to the sanctuary. Kenny looked a little ashen-faced, but Steven said he wanted Dave and Michael to accompany him upstairs now. Up they went and looked around. Dave never entered Sheila's room. Upon their return downstairs, the psychic group decided not to wait and took off throughout the house on their own, asking the tenants to remain in the Dining Room.

"Ok, we have a presence here, no doubt. I'd like to finish up here quickly and get to work. Dave, continue with your story." Judith was taking notes. Dave informed them in detail of the time in Bay Ridge when Mrs. Clark could be heard walking the hall in Jill's apartment. "Oh, well we didn't know about this, now did we Dave?" uttered Harriet, mockingly. "So, Mr. Molloy, that's it. You're still here because you have something to prove!"

"Bullshit," said Dave.

"I guess that's why you ask Dave to accompany you anytime you hear a noise, Harriet," declared Lorena, to the surprise of all. Harriet fell silent, clearly affronted. Rising above herself, she apologized to Dave. "Good," said Steven, "that's it, pull together." The unity of the tenants had been second to none; the presence of the psychic group appeared to have upset the equilibrium.

"Michael?"

"Everyone knows how I feel and what's happened to me, plus I've been with the others for most events. I've nothing to add that you don't know already."

"Hold on," said Dave, are you totally up-to-date to today?"

"Well okay, then just tell us lastly now, a brief synopsis of events since we talked on Tuesday."

Together they filled him in and just to be sure, they threw in anything that may have bearing in their eyes whether the psychic group were fully aware or not. They told them of the outcome of the conversation with the owner; Dave being tripped on the front garden footpath; Lorena's hair being violently yanked in the back garden; Lorena's stone and candle circle in her bedroom; the most recent events in the front room and kitchen; the 4:50am puzzle; the occurrences immediately prior to the priest's arrival; what happened to the priest inside the house; the information the priest relayed to Dave including the possible suicide by hanging in the kitchen; other minor experiences and they saved the worst for last...full details on the unspeakable event in Sheila's bedroom. "You never told me about that!" said an irate Michael. "You didn't need to know about Sheila's horror show," said Harriet. "It would have terrified you; you'd never have come back!"

"Before any séance I want to set up the equipment throughout the house, commence its operation and see where that takes us. We shall conduct further investigation revisiting the results back in our base at Hertfordshire. The séance will probably be conducted tomorrow and Judith shall run that. Tonight we expect to have all the equipment functioning and operational. "Any questions? None?"

"No wait," said Michael, "what type of equipment are you using?"

"A small variety of weapons in our arsenal. Magnetometers, Electric Field Measuring devices, sound equipment stuff, night vision, illuminators, video cameras, that type of thing. Okay then, Kenny and I shall get the gear, no need for anyone to assist us with that and we'll see how we go chaps."

They brought in most of their apparatus and implements and commenced set-up. At first, they targeted the Living Room, Hallway, top of the stairs and Landing. Judith winced when Sheila's door opened and slammed twice right in front of her as she stood on the Landing. Dave noted that she stood defiant, almost unafraid in response to it. They gave notice before starting operations in the Kitchen, allowing time for everyone to get anything they required beforehand. In the midst of this there was banging going on at the front door of the house. It appeared to each of them that it emanated from the inside of the dwelling. It stopped after about 2 minutes, then proceeded again with five loud thumps on the door. Kenny was the main man completing the set-up and once finished he advised everyone they would continue with the rest of the house tomorrow. "Why are you doing this at this point?" asked Dave. "You already have concrete evidence that we have a gigantic presence. You've just lived it for God's sake!" Kenny looked to his boss saying "He has a good argument,

Steven." Steven rubbed his dark short beard, thought for a minute and said "Look Dave, perhaps we are in a habit of going straight to this. We usually don't have other-world interruptions while setting up. Perhaps it is futile in establishing what we appear, as you say, to already know. But we can get printouts from some of this; hard evidence. And the 'Night Vision' may pick up some things we don't see. There should be a lot of spikes, which is a change in electrical current and high electromagnetic field strength usually confirms a spirit. I will suggest however, that we review our strategy in the morning. Meanwhile everyone, until about midnight Judith, Kenny and I shall move about the areas we have now set up in and after that one of us will take a two hour nap or rest. We'll rotate so there will at all times be at least two of us awake and operational. "What about us?" asked Lorena. "I would rather you stayed here in your sanctuary room. If we need you we will call you."

"Suits me," said Michael.

Three more sleeping bags hit the floor. Everyone tried to settle in. But Lorena and Dave became restless and insisted on moving about the house with the English. Their curiosity was aroused. Lorena joined Judith covering the Living Room and Hallway; Dave went upstairs to Kenny and Steven; the kitchen equipment stayed on with nobody present.

11:49pm: Television thrown to the floor in Living Room. Books flew off shelves.

11:50pm: Video camera filmed kitchen rear door flung wide open, its bolt and lock rendered useless.

11:56pm: Dave's mattress in bedroom thrown towards door.

11:56pm: Bathroom door slams, opens, slams.

11:56pm: Sheila's door opens and slams while simultaneously bathroom door repeats movement again.

11:57pm: Video camera in kitchen films cutlery drawer flying open and wrenched from its location, lands across floor.

During these disturbances Judith maintained absolute self-control with some screams coming from Lorena. Kenny left his post and ran downstairs in fright. Dave ran halfway down the flight of stairs but stopped. Steven never budged but was trembling slightly. Michael and Harriet never exited the sanctuary room.

CHAPTER FIFTEEN

SATURDAY, JULY 5TH.

Harriet offered to replace Judith. Steven, now in full battle mode, accepted. Kenny took up duty downstairs with Harriet and Lorena; Dave and Steven kept up with coverage of upstairs. It was undeniable that the entity knew who was there and possibly why.

2:15am: Judith replaces Kenny.

2:36am: Lorena's hair is yanked again and she is thrown to the ground in the hallway. She returns to the Dining Room immediately and vomits. Harriet roars vulgarities at the entity. Michael consoles and assists Lorena.

3:18am: Telephone ripped from its connection, thrown against front door. Harriet removes it to Dining Room. Kenny returns to Living Room.

3:41am: Footsteps on stairs. Steven, Dave, Harriet, Kenny and Judith stare at stairs, see no one while it is ongoing.

4:05am: Dave packs it in and gets in his sleeping bag.

No further disturbances as dawn breaks with everyone in Dining Room jittery and exhausted. They remained there until approximately 10am with not a sound in the house.

All seven went together to the bathroom door for wash and toiletry procedures. Six waited outside. While there, all bedrooms were checked. No damage visible. Equipment was recovered. When the rotation was completed they returned together downstairs without incident. They decided to leave the phone disconnected in the sanctuary room. "Where do we stand at the present moment with everything?" asked Harriet. "The séance is later today, I think," replied Steven. "Hold on, hold everything, surely the séance is a moot point. The way you answered that tells me you're not sure. Let's be honest Steven, you three have been rattled by this house. Something tells me you're not used to this. This is not what you're used to at all! This is something heavier isn't it?"

"Dave, we know what we're doing."

"I didn't say that. What I said was..." *interruption by Judith* "What Dave is implying is that our team is well versed in visiting affected buildings but now we have met our match. I know where you're coming from David but essentially we have not been defeated by our adversary just yet. We may prevail."

"How?" asked Harriet. "The séance, and before you interrupt let me tell you why. He has shown his hand. He hasn't hidden the fact that he's uncontrollably furious and evil at that. Suicide, if that's what it is, has nothing to do with this. The suicide act in his particular case may be a player. But it is not the defining cause of his behavior. It is a factor; a percentage. He appears to have been not a fellow you'd wish to stumble upon in a dark alley encounter in his life before death. Not someone to take home to tea. This knowledge will aid me in how I conduct the séance. He must be challenged and confronted in order for you to achieve any semblance of peace. A gauntlet must be thrown down. Bring him into the open. Take him on. Attempt to expose to him his folly and if that fails drive him out. It has been achieved occasionally in the past."

"That has all the hallmarks of a war," said Dave.

"Are you not in a war?!" declared Judith. Harriet, Lorena and Dave smiled. Michael shuffled. "It is the one last chance you might have. I shall only do it with your blessing and compliance."

"Judith is the maestro at séances," said Steven, "she will guide you through it professionally. As regards listening and measuring gear, we shall now pull back a little from that, but I intend to make good use of camera equipment. I think we require fresh air and a break. Plus I'm famished." Lorena suggested Bewley's in Westmoreland St. in the city centre for breakfast. Off they went, leaving some instruments rolling for now.

They arrived too late for breakfast so lunch it would be. Dave got Harriet back, again! "The men are going to order food fit for savages and I'm sure Lorena and Judith will select appropriately but you dear Harriet, oh, only the Queen's own personal chef shall prepare for you, your Highness. How about you commence with Confit Royal Duck leg, braised red cabbage, braised pearl barley and choose from our selection of carefully-considered gravies to top it off. Following that, perhaps a simple yet exquisite Crème Brulee might round off your luncheon?"

"Mr. Molloy, you've pushed the envelope too far!"

"Apologies, my dearest Harriet, my sincere apologies," a satisfied grin upon his face. Ultimately, the girls had Quiche Lorraine while the men got stuck into Beef & Stout Stew, the English lads taking advantage of the Guinness Stout while in Dublin. "Kenny eats like a horse, we'll have to get him a trough," quipped Michael. Soon they were down to business. "I noticed the Crucifix upon the wall just before the little stairs to the Landing. It's stunning, beautiful in its design and studded with jewels. Gorgeous. Who put it there?" said Judith. "No idea," said Harriet, "it was there when I received the keys to the house."

"It's very large. I figured you had put it there,"

"No Michael, not me."

"It's firmly affixed to the wall. Even if one tries to move it or yanks on it, it is steadfast. Solid to the wall. I suspect we have to assume a previous occupant placed it there for reasons which are evident," said Judith. "It's so beautiful, must have been very expensive," added Lorena. Judith addressed them all. "Are you okay for the séance when we go back?" Dave and Harriet were definite. "Michael?"

"I'm not sure about this. If this doesn't work there is no hope. So, I'll tell you what. I'll come out of my shell and brave this thing BUT that's my last, very last effort." Looking at Lorena, Dave and Harriet "I'm leaving this time permanently if we get no result." Judith turned to Lorena. "What happened to you last night was awful. I understand if you feel you're not up to taking part. I have to impress upon you Lorena however, that you are a central figure in this drama. He gravitates to you. From what you've told us and we have observed, he is either gentle and displays it, albeit highly disturbing for you, or he physically attacks you when unpleased with you. You may be the nerve centre, the nucleus of the present circumstance since you came to Bonaventure Road."

"If I do this and I'm not saying I will, there is something else everyone should know. Oh God, I used a Ouija Board soon after I got to the house, I was by myself just messing around, investigating you might say, curious, I did it alone in my room but I stopped weeks ago. Weeks ago!" Harriet's mouth dropped, clearly annoyed. Dave and Michael were taken by surprise. "Why didn't you tell us Lorena?" said Dave. "Embarrassed; angry at myself, that's why!"

"Did you encounter any response?" asked Judith. "That's the thing, no! Nothing ever happened. I only did it because all this shit was going on. I didn't start this, I can tell you that!"

"That's clear. I thing we all concur on that." Everyone nodded in agreement. "There's something else, was it not you who wanted the séance, who invited them here?!" asked Dave. "I need you in the séance Lorena, you may be pivotal; although the foremost reasons he is in the house have nothing to do with you, but you are currently central."

"My main reason, my main fear is that he'll pull my head back again, I can't handle that."

"I shall sit right beside you, very close to you," said Harriet. "I will sit the other side of you doing the same thing," added Dave. Lorena warmed to that. "I love you two, I wish you'd get along better." The decision had been made. Six would take part with Kenny filming and monitoring the séance in the kitchen. The door would remain open. One white lit candle would be placed in the centre of the table. It would be conducted in daylight. Judith would instruct and advise once everyone was in place and seated. They took two taxis back between them. En route, Judith confided to Dave that as a Medium and paranormal researcher she had attended over 70 hauntings so far and that this was only the third of such magnitude. She described this one as ferocious and she suspected, inherently evil. Of the other two, one had been in the midlands of Ireland and the second was in an old Methodist Church in England. "Did you succeed with the Methodist Church?"

"Yes."

"The Irish one?"

"No."

"Well, here's to victory," said Dave, trying to remain cheerful.

They decided to commence proceedings at 4pm. Dave asked Kenny to log the times anything happened as he expected both his hands would be employed in unison with others. Kenny said he'd try to do his best with that. In the Dining Room Judith addressed those gathered. "Alright, ladies and gentlemen, I shall lead the séance. I will open the process and I want you to stay with my voice, no matter what you see, feel or hear during the proceedings. Fix your senses on me if you are physically struck or touched. Listen to me and do as I say at all times. Do not be afraid. He thrives on that. We are dealing with a Poltergeist and..." She noticed the reaction. "You DO know you are dealing with a Poltergeist, don't you?" After a notable silence Harriet said, "Yes we do. No one had ever used that word before. It's frightening. Terrifying to believe that's what we have. Perhaps that's why we just think of alternative words like ghost or spirit or entity."

"You do have a Poltergeist. They are drawn to water and electricity is their middle name. That is why you saw the pool of water just inside the kitchen door. Some colleagues say a séance is not wise when a Poltergeist is confirmed. I disagree. He must be challenged and defeated. Sent on his merry way. Each of you has proved your strength, your fortitude thus far. Stay the course. Show him your inner mettle, your potency. You have it within you. Do not forget that. I suggest we also keep the back door open to the garden. Let further light and air in. Okay, is everyone set? Kenny, ready to go?" All affirmed their readiness.

They entered the kitchen. They easily pulled open the rear door to the garden as it had barely held after last night's incident. A candle was placed and lit in the centre of the wooden table.

Two extra chairs were brought in. They seated themselves in a circle. Judith sat with her back to the wall to have a clear view of the room. To her right was Harriet, next was Lorena, then Dave, then Steven, Michael and back to Judith. Kenny had audio tapes, video camera and an electrical current instrument ready to activate. He stood in the hall/kitchen doorway. Judith began. "Is everyone relaxed?" Steven nodded and no one answered. The house remained quiet. "Before we start I should like to mention that there is a possibility other spirits could drop in. It is doubtful in this case due to the strength of this fellow but it remains a possibility nonetheless. I suspect he intimidates passing spirits and they may well be afraid of him, but being aware of our process some may try to make contact. Don't concern yourselves with that; that is not what interests us today. Secondly, do not break the circle. It weakens, if not ends the séance. Also the reaction of a Poltergeist can be quite negative to that. Keep your hands held to the person either side of you. Do not let go. If furniture including this table or other items move about, do not be afraid. Keep your hands together, maintain the circle. Keep to my voice. Receive strength from it. Follow along. Stay focused and keep your concentration. Are you all relaxed?" No answer, not even a nod. "Okay Kenny, we're starting."

Her voice strong and clear, she began. "All join hands." She waited a few seconds. "I pray for protection, for everyone here, every person, from beings that would do us harm." Again, a pause. "I want everyone to close their eyes for two minutes. Then you can open them." Pause. "Now, I would like to address the one that is troubling this house. Are you present?" Quietness. "I am addressing the one who troubles this household. Are you present?" Silence. "The one who troubles this house only. Are you present?" Nothing. "Are you..." A jet on the cooker (stove) came on. Kenny turned it off. There were four jets. A second one came on, then a third. Everyone opened their eyes. "I am holding up a Pendulum on a cord. To answer 'Yes' move it back and forth. To answer 'No' move it sideways. Turn it in a circle if your answer is 'I don't know;' do you understand?" Nothing. "Do you understand?" About twelve seconds passed. "Move it back and forth for 'Yes,' sideways for 'No,' do you understand?" A brief few seconds elapsed. The pendulum moved sideways! "Do not mock me. Again, do you understand?" The pendulum moved back and forth. It ceased moving. Then it repeated its movement of back and forth. "Good. Anything I ask you is a yes or no question. Do you understand?" Back and forth the pendulum went. "Are you free to go where you want?" The pendulum swung sideways. "Do you want to leave this house?" It went sideways. "Is there a force trying to pull you from this house?" Back and forth was the reply. "But you do not want to go with that force, is that correct?" The pendulum again swung back and forth. "Have you been here a long time?" The pendulum went in a circle. "Do you have a sense of time, our time?" It moved sideways. 'It is the way of things to move on to where you are supposed to go. Will you accept that and go?" Sideways! "Whatever happened to you, the people who dwell in this house are not responsible for that. Will you leave them in peace?" Sideways! "I am going to let someone else speak. Is that okay?" Back and forth.

She told Lorena to ask the entity to cease the harassing in the house. Lorena: "Please leave me in peace. I am not your enemy. Stop attacking me." Sideways! Judith took back control. "Do you hate the person who just spoke to you?" Sideways. "You must leave this house. It is no longer yours to dwell in. You have to follow..." All four jets ignited on the cooker. The taps turned on and water flowed! The back door slammed closed. People moved in their chairs. She raised her voice as the door continued to open and slam and the water spewed..."YOU HAVE TO FOLLOW THE FORCE THAT CALLS YOU. EVENTUALLY IT SHALL REMOVE YOU FROM HERE. GO! BE WISE. GO!" The candle extinguished. Steven was thrown from his chair. He stayed strong and reseated himself. She kept hold of the pendulum and waited. Kenny turned off the jets. The door stopped moving but stayed shut. The water spew continued. Judith wanted information! "Did someone murder you?" The pendulum moved sideways. "Did you reside in this house?" It swung back and forth ferociously. "Did you die a natural death?" Nothing. She asked again. No movement. Silence. Tumult! Lorena was thrown from her chair as was Harriet. The table rose and crashed to the ground. Dave fell off his chair. Kenny kept filming. Lorena and Harriet were screaming. Michael was vomiting. Judith was on the floor. Dave grabbed Michael and dragged him into the dining room; Steven roared "FUCK YOU" to the entity; as Dave went back for the women, they, Kenny and Steven were pushing him backwards into the Dining Room. They banged the door shut behind them.

The Living Room, kitchen, and upstairs had commotion and ongoing turmoil as the seven of them flopped on the floor of their sanctuary haven. Eventually everything abated and 189 St. Bonaventure Road was still. They sat in ironic solitude.

"Well Judith," said Harriet, "I do believe this completes our tenure in this house."

"I am truly sorry," replied Judith. "I did my best."

"Ireland is not your claim to fame," remarked Dave, "best stick to your Methodist Churches in England!" Then with some afterthought, "Thank you though. Thank you for trying."

"We did succeed in the information department, mates," said Kenny. "He wasn't murdered, he lived here for sure and he's no sense of his time or our time. Also, I picked up massive energy on the instruments, spikes don't even come into it; massive energy! I got a lot of good footage of the table moving and general mayhem too."

"Further to that," said Steven, "Judith ascertained that whatever they are, forces are trying to get him to come to them and he is fighting that off to stay in the house. But I can tell you that's a battle he shall lose. All entities move on, even a vicious Poltergeist like him."

"How long does it take?" Michael inquired. "Well in his dimension, time and space and all that, and although he is relatively in ours, it may seem a short duration. But in our time, it can translate into a few years, often up to three or four centuries. It depends.

"Depends on what?"

"God knows!"

"You'll have to begin your search for new accommodation Harriet."

"I know, Dave."

"Until you find it you can stay with me," said Lorena. "I'm going home to my folks. They like you, you'll be grand."

"Thanks Lorena. I'll take you up on that. What about you Dave?"

"I've had it with flats, apartments, houses for rent, the lot! I'm going back to Coolock. To the family. I'll stay there until this job is finished in Dublin, then it is back to New York for me."

"And I'm back to my Dad's house," said Michael.

"Hold on," said Steven. "There is one last thing we can try."

CHAPTER SIXTEEN

Michael took a good look at Steven. "One last thing we can try? Oh no, no, no. The shit stops here. Unless you'd like to move in yourself?! I'll tell you what, you can take my place!"

"We are at the end of our tether, Steven. We appreciate the time from all three of you and indeed your assistance, but today is our last day here. No more. I agree with Michael, it's too much, too taxing. We can't live like this. It was worth a fight. The fight is over," said Dave. "You haven't heard me out," said Steven, "I am not asking anyone to remain here. We have another ace up our sleeve; one we rarely call into play but I believe now is the time." A 'what now??!' moment beckoned from his listeners. "Will you hear me out?"

"Absolutely not." Michael gathered his belongings together and approached Harriet. He hugged her and embraced Lorena for a somewhat longer period. There were tears in her eyes as Michael turned to Dave and firmly shook his hand. "Goodbye my friend." He bid adieu to all, gave Harriet his keys and departed.

"Before I proceed, I want to restate that I am not expecting any of you to remain. We can instigate this plan today and leave within the hour." They were intrigued. "There is a gentleman in England that some paranormal groups liaise with at times. I know him personally. I have utilized him thus far on one occasion. He is a Minister of the cloth. A Presbyterian minister. Actually he is an Irishman but has been in England many years. An older man. He possesses a successful record in ridding poltergeists and demons from all kinds of buildings. Mind you, he is not one hundred percent victorious but no one comes close to him in this field! He may help you. He refuses to become involved unless other measures have already been attempted. He strictly tackles demonic and evil forces. Nothing else. He is quite skilled. Meticulous, religious, stringent. He doesn't take every case; anyway he has his own regular daily duties to perform. But if he's interested in this particular case, why not? We have all the ingredients here. I can speak to him on this. There is a high probability he'll bite."

"So we could walk out of here today even if he's coming?"

"Yes David,"

"He would have to be here this calendar month. July. We are damn well not paying for August. As it is, we have already paid for July but we cannot guarantee him entry after the 31st. July," said Harriet. "Is it worth doing?" said Lorena, "we are skedaddling out of here today!"

"You can go about your business right now. Carry on with your lives elsewhere. I'll contact him tomorrow at some point, have a chat with him about it; if he agrees I'll give you a call. We can then settle a date to meet here. He'll call the date and time though. I'll impress upon him we just have July to work with."

"It would give me great satisfaction to see him defeated," said Dave. 'What do you think girls?"

Harriet concurred. "I am on board fully. But again, I leave here today and I won't be checking on the house in the interim." She glanced at Lorena.

"I can't leave you two. You are right. '*Dwellers in Darkness*,' do you know what that means to me?" mused Lorena. "It is a book. A book's title and that title reminds me of the intricacies of this house. We are dwelling in darkness. Not so much in our house. The good dwelling in the darkness represents us and the bad is the darkness and it's HIM! We are intertwined in a strange and eerie way. It clouds everything. I want birds to sing, the sun to shine, the trees to bloom in our garden. Our garden of light, our house. He is a perverted convoluted presence slithering like a snake into our minds. I have seen what he has done to Michael and Sheila and to us. We will never be the same again. Yes, I want this dead evil fucker to lose. I want him destroyed!"

"Jesus, Lorena! Holy shit." Dave stood riveted. Lorena was herself again. Her philosophical self, wrapped in an array of sensibilities, perception, albeit offbeat. She too had changed. Damaged in the loveliness of her. The benevolence of her. A charismatic poetic soul in the clutches of a foul and unholy entity. Yet a soul that remained divine in such dark circumstance. "Bravo Lorena," exclaimed Steven. "Alright, we'll get cracking then."

They packed up as Dave assisted the team with their Hard Equipment Cases and tripods. Telephone numbers were rechecked. Kenny said goodbye to Dave and the girls as he wouldn't be required in the presence of the Protestant Minister. Apparently the pastor enforced a rule: "No gadgets!" The team headed to a hotel for their last night, dropping off Harriet and Lorena along the way. As Dave's father pulled from the kerb at 189 St. Bonaventure Rd; Dave glanced back. The house had maintained its eerie silence since the events of this afternoon. Had the entity left? Had Judith's stratagems brought the entity food for thought? Dave knew better.

"Are you sure you had a ghost there?"

"Positively, Dad." Dave's father asked no further questions. David Molloy could concentrate on his job now. Relax in his family's home. Lead a normal life pending his one return visit to Clontarf. Something goaded him though. It was a Protestant Minister's help they were seeking. Dave was a devout believer in Catholicism. He held by the Roman Catholic Church with all his heart. He had profound issues with the first seven letters of the word Protestant. 'Isn't that where the name originated? They were and still are by their very existence, protesting against the Mother Church. The Holy Church sustained from the first Pope. St. Peter. Christ's Apostle.' Fully cognizant that there are people in every Christian denomination of good faith, over the next two weeks he came to terms with the expected visit of the gentleman from England, eventually embracing his arrival.

Steven called Lorena. "We are on for the 26th. A Saturday."

"Brilliant! I'll tell the others."

"We're flying in Friday night the 25th. We'll meet you at the house Saturday morning at half past ten. Is that okay?"

"Great. Thanks Steven." Lorena phoned Dave and alerted him. Talking to Harriet that evening she said, "You know Harriet, I do think that Steven fella just loves all this shit. He lives for it."

"Easy for him." said Harriet. "He lives FOR it, not IN it!"

SATURDAY, JULY 26TH.

"Where's Lorena?" It was the morning of destiny, the last hope in their battle for peace. Dave looked at his watch. 10:15am. The Sycamore trees cast their branches above Harriet and Dave's lowly heads, the sun obstructed by a vast dark green reproach of foliage as they stood at the railings outside the house. Two figures in the shadows, yet central to the drama. "We had a call this morning from Steven. They don't want Lorena here. Specifically, the Minister's request. It must have something to do with how the entity reacts to her. I don't know. Perhaps he feels it will inflame the situation."

"So he thinks he has a better chance without Lorena here? Better odds of success?"

"Apparently."

"How does Lorena feel about that?"

"Not good, Dave. She's in the middle of all this almost from the start and it doesn't sit well with her. She says she belongs here with us and frankly I know where she's coming from."

"It's not quite the same without her, is it? She's probably more fortunate not to be here though, the way this crap goes down!"

"Definitely."

A car pulled up. Out stepped Steven, Judith and a rather refined-looking gentleman who appeared to be aged in his early sixties, of tall and good build with broad shoulders, well presented in a shirt, tie, sports jacket and trousers. He walked towards them with excellent posture and comportment as Steven did the introductions. "This is Harriet and Dave; chaps, this is Gordon." No surname was offered nor announced. "Thank you for coming," said Dave. Although Steven had alluded to his Irishness, Gordon spoke with a cultured English accent. "You're welcome." He had an air of authority about him. He conversed slowly. "Now, what I should like to do is enter the premises alone for a minute. I must insist that each of you remains here by the gate as I step into the garden. I shall summon you presently." Harriet began to offer him the keys when Steven placed his hand gently over hers and whispered "No need, not yet. And don't worry, he is well-briefed."

Gordon, in a meticulous manner and looking straight ahead, walked inchmeal up the garden path; then turned at a crisp right angle onto the grass. He strolled into the centre of the front garden and turned to face the facade of the house. With his back to the others and not moving, he kept his gaze forward, occasionally glancing upwards to the front bedrooms. Approximately two minutes elapsed. Then, without turning around he said, "Please unlock and open the door. I shall enter first." Dave took his own keys, opened the front door and stepped back. "We shall all enter. You shall stay behind me in the hallway and shut the door once we are inside. Stay by the door. Do not talk or interfere."

Standing in the quiet house he removed a small Bible from his pocket. He spoke loudly with conviction. "I am here for the Glory of God. I speak in His Holy Name. I am here not to bargain or negotiate. You insult the Glory of the Almighty. Be gone!" He took out anointing oil. He read a few lines from his Bible. He walked into the Living Room. They heard him command "Get out in the name of Jesus. I invite the Holy Spirit into this dwelling; into all its parts.

Get out in the name of Jesus. I invite the Holy Spirit into this dwelling." They heard something fall in the room. The four of them went to have a look. As they arrived and peeked in, they saw the Minister being hit on the head by a bookshelf sprung from the wall! The T.V. was already upon the carpet. Gordon didn't budge. "I CALL ON THE HOLY SPIRIT TO ENTER THIS DWELLING. GET OUT IN THE NAME OF JESUS." The television rose in the air and flew at him. He jumped out of its way. He anointed the mirror, the bay window and the fireplace. Banging could be heard from upstairs. He stayed the course. "GET OUT IN THE NAME OF JESUS." He entered the Dining Room. He repeated everything. He had no response there. He entered the Kitchen. There was blood on his face. "I INVITE THE HOLY SPIRIT INTO THIS DWELLING." The house erupted. The entire residence exploded in a detonation of turmoil. "I AM NEITHER HERE TO BARGAIN OR NEGOTIATE. YOU INSULT THE GLORY OF GOD. GET OUT AND BE GONE!" The jets on the stove, the back door, the taps over the sink, all in motion. A flying chair was cast at his back. He fell forward. He regained himself. "I PLEAD THE BLOOD OF JESUS

OVER EVERY INCH OF THIS DWELLING." A pool of water emanated from under the skirting board. "I AM NEITHER HERE TO BARGAIN OR NEGOTIATE. I AM HERE FOR THE GLORY OF GOD." Through the noise and danger he commenced his journey upstairs, praying as he went. They followed him. At the top of the stairs the Crucifix came away from the wall, rotated upside down and returned transfixed to the wall. He repeated his commands in Dave's room. He stepped into the bathroom. The toilet flushed; the shower went on; the whole house was in loud agitation. He ignored everything around him and proceeded up the shorter stairs to the Landing. Harriet ran from the house. As Dave, Judith and Steven followed him, the toilet seat was ripped from its position and flew like a Frisbee through the open bathroom door at them. Dave was struck in the mouth, falling down, stunned and bleeding. Judith was hit in the shoulder as the toilet seat continued its journey. Gordon never looked back. He entered Sheila's room. "I PLEAD THE BLOOD OF..." Steven attested that the mattress from Sheila's bed rose and pushed Gordon to the wall. The mattress then eased and fell." I PLEAD THE BLOOD OF JESUS

OVER EVERY INCH OF THIS DWELLING, OVER EVERY PERSON LIVING HERE. THE GLORY OF GOD PREVAILS." The house shook with rage. He entered Harriet's room. "GET OUT IN THE NAME OF JESUS." Amidst all the clamour he went downstairs praying and commanding aloud and walked through the kitchen to the back garden. "I INVITE THE HOLY SPIRIT INTO THIS DWELLING; INTO ALL ITS PARTS." Walking back in, he told them to go outside to the front of the house. They did so. He followed but just inside the entrance, he turned to face the house and declared "I ASK THE ALMIGHTY FATHER TO SANCTIFY AND SEAL THIS HOUSE." He then closed the door.

Harriet was seated outside on the path, her back against the railing. She was white as a sheet. Dave had never seen her like this. Not Harriet. He sat down with her, putting his arm around her. She leaned, rested her head upon his shoulder. Blood was still seeping from Dave's mouth. Gordon approached them. Looking down at them, he said, "I shall pray for you. You indeed have been demonstrably brave and I dare say always have been in your suffering here. There is no need to be tormented any longer. I believe God has you in the palm of HIS hand."

He walked to the car and sat in the back seat. Steven closed the gate to the house. "Where's the nearest pharmacy?" Dave told him. "Stay there, I'll be back. Judith, stay with them."

He returned shortly afterward and insisted on cleaning Dave's wound. Judith had no broken bones but was still in shock. Steven helped her to the front passenger seat. "Can I drive you chaps home?"

"No thanks," said Harriet, "I think we'll just sit here for a moment."

CHAPTER SEVENTEEN

FRIDAY, AUGUST 29TH.

The restaurant inside Dublin's Clarence Hotel on Wellington Quay was hopping with customers as waiters and waitresses bustled about with Soup du Jour, fresh fish and all miscellany of hot concoctions for the ravished clientele. Established in 1852 and still retaining its rustic charm and old Dublin atmosphere, the hotel was an impromptu suitable setting for the three young persons at the table.

"So, fill me in, how are you two?"

"Oh, what a difference Dave, flying free and happy these days."

"You look great Lorena and do you Harriet, as always."

"Well," exclaimed Harriet, "I think I'll have one of your specials Dave, a great big good old-fashioned American cheese burger." They broke into laughter. "It's great to see you two getting along. How are you Dave? How have you been keeping?"

"It takes time Lorena, doesn't it? It was a hell of a nightmare."

"'Hell' is the right word for it. If we're honest, it will take us a while to recover. But you can keep your therapy groups. They'd deny the existence of the supernatural just as some of them deny God. One goes with the other. The truth is we can never talk about it with anyone really, except amongst ourselves."

"Therapy Groups? Oh, please! We'll live with it," said Harriet. "Do you think Gordon cleaned the house, Dave?"

"I hope so. We'll never really know, will we? Unless we go back."

"A Poltergeist! Why is it that during all that time, we never called it what it was?" asked Lorena.

"I've considered that," said Harriet. "We loved that house. I suspect that if we lived anywhere else, we would have cleared out promptly. The house drew us in, dare I say like a Love Affair. You find yourself enticed into it and you cannot extract yourself from it. It is clear that the word 'Poltergeist' and our Love Affair could never complement each other. Yet they merged closer together in an ironic way. Then they clashed like lightning, and thunder ensued. And so here we sit."

"You never cease to amaze me, Harriet."

"Ah shut up Dave."

"So you're still together in Cabra?"

"For the moment," said Lorena. "Harriet's off to greener pastures, aren't you Harriet darling?"

"Yes I am. I have a job interview at home in Limerick City. Advertising. With the experience I've garnered I should have a chance. If I get it, I go."

"Whatever happens, let's all stay in touch," said Lorena.

"Good God, most definitely," said Dave.

"Always," agreed Harriet. "Always."

THURSDAY, MARCH 13TH. 2014.

Eddie O'Leary's Volvo circled higher, elevating itself in the Multi-Storey Short Term Parking Garage at Dublin International Airport. "There's no roof at the top, last chance for a smoke, Dave." A cold brisk air enveloped them as they alighted the car. Dave put his hand in his pocket and pulling a Carroll's cigarette, lit up. Gazing up at the cloudy Irish skies, he blew a puff of smoke into the air. 'The same brand Michael used to smoke,' crossed his mind. Life had changed him those 28 years ago; he had taken up the smoking and never looked back. Now he struggled to cease. "How long until you get to Florida?"

"Ah, about eight hours to New York and then a three hour flight down to Tampa. A 90 minute layover. You get used to it."

Inside Terminal 2 Eddie shook his hand. "Look after yourself my old friend, until we meet again. Tell the wife and family I said hello."

"Thanks for everything Eddie. Take care of yourself on those city roads. It's a dangerous world these days driving a taxi in Dublin. Be careful."

"Will do."

As Dave walked through the terminal his eyes caught the check-in desks one last time. He thought he saw Lorena, checking the bags and the passports, her beautiful smile greeting the passengers. But that was wishful thinking and he knew it. She was long gone into the mists of time. Memories that had returned to him in such poignancy through Eddie's inquisitiveness and their consequential visit to 189 St. Bonaventure Road, just two nights earlier.

As the big Aer Lingus Boeing 747-100 took to the skies and headed across Ireland out above the Atlantic, Dave tried to focus on the life he had made in America. He was returning to his wife, his son and daughter, both young adults now; and the company he had built from humble beginnings in the world of Market Research and Political Opinion Polls. But the memory of St. Bonaventure Road those many years ago, so intensely revisited less than 48 hours before, stood poised, engulfing his mind.

'Not a Blackbird or Robin ever sang. A Victorian house with a 1940's past. How strange. That poor priest who had no warning. He helped me nevertheless. God be with him, he couldn't have been older than my son is now. The séance. What did it achieve? If anything. Oh, but they were brave and Judith gave it her best shot. And Kenny with his cameras and all sorts of gizmos.' His face broadened with a smile. 'But most of all, that minister.' "Tea or Coffee, sir?"

"Oh, sorry, yes, I'll have a coffee; milk, no sugar."

'Yes, that Protestant Minister. Walking through the house courageous in the face of evil, defiant; God, he inspired me if the truth be known; don't know if he succeeded or not, we were never going back there, but he was a symbol of all that is just, all that is good in this confusing world; yes, I have to admit he changed my view of other denominations. Are we not all Christian? Does God Himself discriminate when one man stands up in His Name and calls out a demon or poltergeist? No, He doesn't. That man was a soldier of God!'

'And what of Lorena and Michael and Harriet? And poor Sheila. Who could fault her? She endured the most. What did that bastard have against HER? We'll never know.' He browsed the catalogue in the seat pocket in front of him. 'Look at them. Companies selling jewelry and perfumes and expensive watches and so forth. What do they know?! What do all these people sitting here on this plane know about such things as dimensions and demons and poltergeists?

They rush their children to school, run errands, argue, laugh and play in their busy lives. What do they know? They don't want to know! Or they don't believe. Just as I once did.'

'There are no answers for the common man. Perhaps there are not supposed to be. Society ridicules the few who say they have experienced this. They mock because they fear. It's like the man on his deathbed who has been a declared atheist all his life and lived by that ethos. In his dying breaths he fears God and turns to Him or begs for mercy. Such is the way it is. But what did we achieve by staying there in that house? What did we accomplish? Did we fight our terror to prove a point? Oh, I don't know. What I do know is I have become a better man for it, strengthened internally and motivated to be cognizant that we must live our lives with open minds and a good heart. For goodness and evil do exist and they are the mortal enemies of each other in this world and the universe, in dimensions of time and space. I am witness to that.'

As the flight crossed the first time zone, he recalled the parting words of Lorena in the Clarence Hotel, that night in August 1986. "It was never a losing battle, Dave. We responded to hatred with love. We responded to evil with good. And because we are better souls for it, we won! That is what we did."

AFTERWORD

HARRIET moved to England in 1991. She formed her own advertising firm; married with children she resides there to this day.

MICHAEL retired from Dublin Bus not long ago. He has stayed in contact with Dave over the years. He never married.

LORENA furthered her education and changed career having studied to become a Psychotherapist. She continues to practice her profession in Dublin.

DAVE returned to New York in 1987 and relocated to Florida some years later. He has since retired.

Little is known of Sheila.

ABOUT THE AUTHOR

DEREK MEYLER is the author of *Variations* and the critically-acclaimed *The Irishman's Journey to Montana*. An established writer, orator and Speechwriter for various politicians, he studied at O'Connell School in his native Dublin. He currently resides in County Wexford, Ireland.

Printed in Poland
by Amazon Fulfillment
Poland Sp. z o.o., Wrocław

62281903R00148